SIGNS

31 UNDENIABLE PROPHECIES OF THE APOCALYPSE

VOLUME 2

DR. DAVID JEREMIAH

Turning Point
with Dr. David Jeremiah

© 2019, Oct. 2021, Turning Point for God
P.O. Box 3838
San Diego, CA 92163
All Rights Reserved

Unless otherwise indicated, Scripture verses quoted are taken from the NEW KING JAMES VERSION.

Printed in the United States of America.

Contents

About Dr. David Jeremiah and Turning Point 4

How to Use This Study Guide 5

Introduction 11

Part 3: International Signs

12. Rapture: "The Rapture of the Redeemed" 13

13. Resurrection: "The Ultimate
    'Extreme Makeover'" 27

14. Heaven: "What's Up With Heaven" 41

15. Judgment Seat of Christ:
    "The Pretenders" 53

16. Rewards: "Heaven's Oscars" 67

17. Worship: "Worship in Heaven" 81

Part 4: Cultural Signs

18. Four Riders: "The Four Horsemen
    of the Apocalypse" 93

19. Antichrist: "The Beast From the Sea" 105

20. False Prophet: "The Beast From the Earth" . . . 117

21. Martyrs: "The Martyrs" 129

Resources 142

Stay Connected 144

ABOUT DR. DAVID JEREMIAH AND TURNING POINT

Dr. David Jeremiah is the founder of Turning Point, a ministry committed to providing Christians with sound Bible teaching relevant to today's changing times through radio and television broadcasts, audio series, books, and live events. Dr. Jeremiah's common-sense teaching on topics such as family, prayer, worship, angels, and biblical prophecy forms the foundation of Turning Point.

David and his wife, Donna, reside in El Cajon, California, where he serves as the senior pastor of Shadow Mountain Community Church. David and Donna have four children and twelve grandchildren.

In 1982, Dr. Jeremiah brought the same solid teaching to San Diego television that he shares weekly with his congregation. Shortly thereafter, Turning Point expanded its ministry to radio. Dr. Jeremiah's inspiring messages can now be heard worldwide on radio, television, and the Internet.

Because Dr. Jeremiah desires to know his listening audience, he travels nationwide holding ministry rallies that touch the hearts and lives of many people. According to Dr. Jeremiah, "At some point in time, everyone reaches a turning point; and for every person, that moment is unique, an experience to hold onto forever. There's so much changing in today's world that sometimes it's difficult to choose the right path. Turning Point offers people an understanding of God's Word as well as the opportunity to make a difference in their lives."

Dr. Jeremiah has authored numerous books, including *Escape the Coming Night* (Revelation), *The Handwriting on the Wall* (Daniel), *Overcoming Loneliness*, *God in You* (Holy Spirit), *When Your World Falls Apart*, *31 Days to Happiness—Searching for Heaven on Earth*, *Captured by Grace*, *I Never Thought I'd See the Day!*, *Agents of the Apocalypse*, *RESET—Ten Steps to Spiritual Renewal*, *Ten Questions Christians Are Asking*, *A Life Beyond Amazing*, and *Overcomer*.

How to Use This Study Guide

The purpose of this Turning Point study guide is to reinforce Dr. David Jeremiah's dynamic, in-depth teaching and to aid the reader in applying biblical truth to his or her daily life. This study guide is designed to be used in conjunction with Dr. Jeremiah's *Signs* audio series, but it may also be used by itself for personal or group study.

Structure of the Lessons

Each lesson is based on one of the messages in the *Signs* compact disc series and focuses on specific passages in the Bible. Each lesson is composed of the following elements:

- *Outline*

The outline at the beginning of the lesson gives a clear, concise picture of the topic being studied and provides a helpful framework for readers as they listen to Dr. Jeremiah's teaching.

- *Overview*

The overview summarizes Dr. Jeremiah's teaching on the passage being studied in the lesson. Readers should refer to the Scripture passages in their own Bibles as they study the overview. Unless otherwise indicated, Scripture verses quoted are taken from the New King James Version.

- *Personal and Group Application Questions*

This section contains a variety of questions designed to help readers dig deeper into the lesson and the Scriptures, and to apply the lesson to their daily lives. For Bible study groups or Sunday school classes, these questions will provide a springboard for group discussion and interaction.

- *Did You Know?*

This section presents a fascinating fact, historical note, or insight that adds a point of interest to the preceding lesson.

Personal Study

Thank you for selecting *Signs* for your current study. The lessons in this study guide were created to help you gain fresh insights into God's Word and develop new perspectives on topics you may have previously studied. Each lesson is designed to challenge your thinking, and help you grow in your knowledge of Christ. During your study, it is our prayer that you will discover how biblical truth affects every aspect of your life and your relationship with Christ will be strengthened.

When you commit to completing this study guide, try to set aside a time, daily or weekly, to read through the lessons without distraction. Have your Bible nearby when you read the study guide, so you're ready to look up verses if you need to. If you want to use a notebook to write down your thoughts, be sure to have that handy as well. Take your time to think through and answer the questions. If you plan on reading the study guide with a small group, be sure to read ahead and be prepared to take part in the weekly discussions.

Leader's Guide

Thank you for your commitment to lead a group through *Signs*. Being a leader has its own rewards. You may discover that your walk with the Lord deepens through this experience. Throughout the study guide, your group will explore new topics and review study questions that encourage thought-provoking group discussion.

The lessons in this study guide are suitable for Sunday school classes, small-group studies, elective Bible studies, or home Bible study groups. Each lesson is structured to provoke thought and help you grow in your knowledge and understanding of God. There are multiple components in this section that can help you structure your lessons and discussion time, so make sure you read and consider each one.

Before You Begin

Before you begin each meeting, make sure you and your group are well-versed with the content of the chapter. Every person should have his or her own study guide so they can follow along and write in the study guide if need be. When possible, the study guide should be used with the corresponding compact disc series. You may wish to assign the study guide lesson as homework prior to the meeting of the group and then use the meeting time to listen to the CD and discuss the lesson.

To ensure that everyone has a chance to participate in the discussion, the ideal size for a group is around eight to ten people. If there are more than ten people, try to break up the bigger group into smaller subgroups. Make sure the members are committed to participating each week, as this will help create stability and help you better prepare the structure of the meeting.

At the beginning of the study each week, start the session with a question to challenge group members to think about the issues you will be discussing. The members can answer briefly, but the goal is to have an idea in their mind as you go over the lesson. This allows the group members to become engaged and ready to interact with the group.

After reviewing the lesson, try to initiate a free-flowing discussion. Invite group members to bring questions and insights they may have discovered to the next meeting, especially if they were unsure of the meaning of some parts of the lesson. Be prepared to discuss how biblical truth applies to the world we live in today.

Weekly Preparation

As the group leader, here are a few things you can do to prepare for each meeting:

- Choose whether or not you will play the CD message during your small group session.

  If you decide to play the CD message from Dr. Jeremiah as part of the meeting, you will need to adjust the group time accordingly.

- Make sure you are thoroughly familiar with the material in the lesson.

  Make sure you understand the content of the lesson so you know how to structure group time and you are prepared to lead group discussion.

- Decide, ahead of time, which questions you plan to discuss.

  Depending on how much time you have each week, you may not be able to reflect on every question. Select specific questions which you feel will evoke the best discussion.

- Take prayer requests.

  At the end of your discussion, take prayer requests from your group members and pray for each other.

How to Use This Study Guide • 7

Structuring the Discussion Time

If you need help in organizing your time when planning your group Bible study, here are two schedules, for sixty minutes and ninety minutes, which can give you a structure for the lesson:

Option 1 (Listen to Audio CD)	60 Minutes	90 Minutes
Welcome: Members arrive and get settled.	N/A	5 minutes
Getting Started Question: Prepares the group for interacting with one another.	Welcome and Getting Started 5 minutes	15 minutes
Message: Listen to the audio CD.	40 minutes	40 minutes
Discussion: Discuss group study questions.	10 minutes	25 minutes
Prayer and Application: Final application for the week and prayer before dismissal.	5 minutes	5 minutes

Option 2 (No Audio CD)	60 Minutes	90 Minutes
Welcome: Members arrive and get settled.	5 minutes	10 minutes
Getting Started Question: Prepares the group for interacting with one another.	10 minutes	10 minutes
Message: Review the lesson.	15 minutes	25 minutes
Discussion: Discuss group study questions.	25 minutes	35 minutes
Prayer and Application: Final application for the week and prayer before dismissal.	5 minutes	10 minutes

As the group leader, it is up to you to keep track of the time and keep things moving along according to your schedule. If your group is having a good discussion, don't feel the need to stop and move on to the next question. Remember, the purpose is to pull together ideas, and share unique insights on the lesson. Make time each week to discuss how to apply these truths to living for Christ today.

The purpose of discussion is for everyone to participate, but don't be concerned if certain group members are more quiet—they may be internally reflecting on the questions and need time to process their ideas before they can share them.

Group Dynamics

Leading a group study can be a rewarding experience for you and your group members—but that doesn't mean there won't be challenges. Certain members may feel uncomfortable discussing topics that they consider very personal, and might be afraid of being called on. Some members might have disagreements on specific issues. To help prevent these scenarios, consider the following ground rules:

- If someone has a question that may seem off topic, suggest that it is discussed at another time, or ask the group if they are okay with addressing that topic.
- If someone asks a question you don't know the answer to, confess that you don't know and move on. If you feel comfortable, invite other group members to give their opinions, or share their comments based on personal experience.
- If you feel like a couple of people are talking much more than others, direct questions to people who may not have shared yet. You could even ask the more dominating members to help draw out the quiet ones.
- When there is a disagreement, encourage the group members to process the matter in love. Invite members from opposing sides to evaluate their opinions and consider the ideas of the other members. Lead the group through Scripture that addresses the topic, and look for common ground.

When issues arise, remind your group to think of Scripture: "Love one another" (John 13:34), "If it is possible, as much as depends on you, live peaceably with all men" (Romans 12:18), and "Be quick to listen, slow to speak and slow to become angry" (James 1:19, NIV).

For Continuing Study

For a complete listing of Dr. Jeremiah's materials for personal and group study call 1-800-947-1993, go online to www.DavidJeremiah.org, or write to Turning Point, P.O. Box 3838, San Diego, CA 92163.

Dr. Jeremiah's *Turning Point* program is currently heard or viewed around the world on radio, television, and the Internet in English. *Momento Decisivo*, the Spanish translation of Dr. Jeremiah's messages, can be heard on radio in every Spanish speaking country in the world. The television broadcast is also broadcast by satellite throughout the Middle East with Arabic subtitles.

Contact Turning Point for radio and television program times and stations in your area, or visit our website at www.DavidJeremiah.org/stationlocator.

SIGNS
VOLUME 2

INTRODUCTION

When we discuss biblical and prophetic signs, it is important to note that they are not all expressed and exhibited in the same manner. Some of the signs we encounter in the Bible are purely informational. Others are invitational, and still others offer warnings about the road ahead—warnings that apply to both our present and future. All of these signs are important, and none should be ignored.

Every Christian should be motivated deep in their hearts to understand and apply the truths communicated through the prophetic signs of Scripture. Why? Because it is important to God! The Bible dedicates more space to the subject of prophecy than any other. In fact, there are over twelve hundred prophecies in God's Word just concerning the first and second coming of Jesus Christ!

Jesus Himself talked about signs verifying His first coming, signs foretelling His second coming, and signs outlining both specific and general elements of the end of the age. Most importantly, Jesus told us to keep our eyes open so that we would not be caught unaware as the signs of the times indicate that the end is indeed near. And when Jesus told us to open our eyes, He did so to encourage us to focus not just on the coming ills, but primarily to gaze upon Him—the Prince of Peace.

As the end of the world culminates with all spiritual and physical matter coming together in a great cacophony, it should come as no surprise that heavenly signs and elements weigh deeply into the story of the coming of the end of the age. Recall that in the last study guide, we likened end-time events as a five-act play.

So as we enter into the second study guide of this series, we now find ourselves in the third and central act of this story. The previous two acts dealt with earthly realities, but as we reach the middle of this saga, the story shifts upward at all the heavenly signs of the end. And with this turn toward the heavenly, a glimmer of hope now arrives.

It all starts with the Rapture of the Church as described by the apostle Paul in 1 Thessalonians 4:16: "For the Lord Himself will descend from heaven with a shout, with the voice of an archangel, and with the trumpet of God." Just imagine the stunning and sensational scene that will one day appear in the sky: Jesus Christ descending from heaven with all power and authority. What a day that will be!

But that is only the beginning. The Rapture will immediately encompass the resurrection of dead believers and the transformation of living believers. This is Christ calling His Church to be with Him forever. At that point, Jesus will escort all of them to heaven—a place so perfect and divine that we have no comprehension of its glory. There in heaven all the saints will experience the Judgment Seat of Christ where rewards for faithful service will be handed out. After that, a praise and worship celebration unlike anything ever witnessed on earth will commence.

Following that heavenly scene, our play comes to the fourth act, the climax of the story—a time known as the Tribulation. The Tribulation is a future seven-year period during which unspeakable horrors will be unleashed upon the world. This is a world devoid of all Christian influence. You do not want to be on the planet at this moment of time.

The Tribulation also features some of the most infamous characters in all of Scripture: Satan, the Antichrist, and the False Prophet. People often think that these are manifestations of the same person, but they are all distinct, and after concluding this study, you will know the role that each will play as the End Times unfold on planet Earth.

LESSON 12

Rapture
The Rapture of the Redeemed

1 Thessalonians 4:13-18

In this lesson we define and discover the details of the coming event known as the Rapture.

OUTLINE

As He prepared to leave this world, Jesus told His disciples He would return and take them to the place He had prepared for them. Later, the apostle Paul provided the details of this event. Since it could happen at any time, the Rapture is a strong motivation for a consecrated, expectant life.

   I.   **The Rapture Is a Signless Event**

  II.   **The Rapture Is a Surprise Event**

 III.   **The Rapture Is a Sudden Event**

  IV.   **The Rapture Is a Selective Event**

   V.   **The Rapture Is a Spectacular Event**

  VI.   **The Rapture Is a Sequential Event**
        A. The Return
        B. The Resurrection
        C. The Redemption
        D. The Rapture and the Reunion

 VII.   **The Rapture Is a Strengthening Event**
        A. Expectation
        B. Consecration
        C. Examination

OVERVIEW

Two publishing events have helped insert the Rapture of the Church into cultural conversations around the world. First was *The Late Great Planet Earth*, written by Hal Lindsey, and released in 1970.

The second event was the twelve-volume series of books known as "The Left Behind Series," *Left Behind* being the title of the first volume that was released in 1995. The books were co-authored by Tim LaHaye and Jerry Jenkins. The ninth volume, *Desecration*, was released shortly after the terror attacks of September 11, 2001, and sold enough copies before the end of 2001 to be the world's bestselling book of that year.

These authors have done the Church a great service by reminding her of the incredible importance of the prophetic Scriptures. The Rapture is perhaps the most important piece of prophecy for today's Christians to understand since it could very well impact them personally.

In this lesson, we will discover what the Rapture is, defend it biblically, and explain its personal and practical importance for the Christian.

In summary, the Rapture is an event where all who have put their trust in Christ, living and deceased, will suddenly be caught up from earth, be joined with Christ in the air, and taken to heaven. Paul describes the Rapture in 1 Thessalonians 4:13-18.

"Rapture" is not a biblical word. It is derived from the Latin translation of 1 Thessalonians 4:17, which translates Greek *harpazo* (to catch up or carry away) as *rapiemur* from the Latin *rapio*. The Greek *harpazo* occurs fourteen times in the New Testament with four variations of meaning, each of which contributes to understanding what Paul is describing in verse 17: "Then we who are alive *and* remain shall be caught up together with [the dead] in the clouds to meet the Lord in the air."

First, *harpazo* can mean "to carry off by force." Christ will use His power to remove living and deceased believers from the last enemy, death.

Second, *harpazo* can mean "to claim for oneself eagerly." Christ purchased us with His blood and so will return to claim those who are His.

Third, *harpazo* can mean "to snatch away speedily." The Rapture will occur "in the twinkling of an eye" (1 Corinthians 15:52).

Fourth, *harpazo* can mean "to rescue from the danger of destruction." This meaning supports the idea that the Rapture will save the Church from the danger of the seven-year Tribulation.

This coming event is part one of Christ's two-part return to earth. First, to remove the Church from the world. Second, seven years later, to establish His kingdom on earth. For every prophecy in Scripture about Christ's first advent there are eight about His second.[1] The 260 chapters of the New Testament contain 318 references to the Second Coming of Christ.[2]

Will the Rapture occur at Christ's Second Coming? The short answer is, "Yes, but...." The Rapture sets in motion the end-time events leading to Christ's Second Coming. The two stages—Rapture and Return—will be separated by a seven-year Tribulation on earth. The purpose of the Rapture is to spare Christ's own from the horrors of the Tribulation according to Revelation 3:10.

The physical return of Christ will happen at the end of the Tribulation as described in vivid detail in Revelation 19. The apostle John's vision of Christ's return echoes what Zechariah saw in the Old Testament: a giant battle, Christ returning to the Mount of Olives, bringing His saints with Him (Zechariah 14:1, 3-5). Jude states what will happen when Christ returns: judgment of the ungodly (Jude 14-15).

The prophets saw what appears to be the Tribulation—"the time of Jacob's trouble" (Jeremiah 30:7)—not the Rapture. But that is not surprising; they didn't differentiate clearly between the First and Second Advents of Christ. The prophets "inquired and searched carefully" (1 Peter 1:10-11) but saw more of the big picture than the details. And they didn't see the Church at all, which is who the Rapture affects. The prophets saw the future like seeing successive mountain peaks through a telephoto lens. They saw the peaks (events), but not the distance that separates them.

Three New Testament passages tell us about the Rapture: John 14:1-3; 1 Corinthians 15:50-57; 1 Thessalonians 4:13-18. Paul's words in 1 Thessalonians are the most complete and form the basis for this lesson.

First, we must note that Paul gained his understanding of the Rapture via special revelation from God—he called it a "mystery" in 1 Corinthians 15:51, meaning a truth not previously revealed. The revelation was "by the word of the Lord" (1 Thessalonians 4:15).

Second, Paul passed on the content of this revelation to meet a practical concern of the Christians in Thessalonica. They were concerned about the fate of Christians who died before Christ's

The Rapture of the Redeemed • 15

Second Coming (1 Thessalonians 4:13-18) and about the timing of the Rapture—whether it had already happened (2 Thessalonians 2:1-2).

Now, seven characteristics of the Rapture.

THE RAPTURE IS A SIGNLESS EVENT

Unlike the Second Coming, no signs will precede the Rapture. It could occur at any moment. This is called the doctrine of *imminency* —that is, the Rapture is imminent; it could happen at any moment. Specifically, nothing in God's prophetic program must take place as a prerequisite to the Rapture. Things *may* happen but nothing *must* happen. That means we don't know when it could happen. It could be today or years from today.

Bible expositor A. T. Pierson wrote, "Imminence is the combination of two conditions, viz., certainty and uncertainty. By an imminent event we mean one which is certain to occur at some time, uncertain at what time."[3]

Without any warning, Jesus Christ will return to rapture His saints and take them to heaven. Christians must live prepared lives, ready to meet their Savior at any moment.

THE RAPTURE IS A SURPRISE EVENT

While many through the years have predicted the date of the Rapture and Jesus' Second Coming, Jesus' words in Matthew 24:36-39 should be taken literally: No one, including Jesus and the angels, knows the time of His return. Only God the Father knows. Not knowing when Jesus will come for His Church causes us to be ready at all times.

THE RAPTURE IS A SUDDEN EVENT

Paul wrote that the Rapture will take place "in a moment in the twinkling of an eye" (1 Corinthians 15:52). "Twinkling" likely refers to the amount of time it takes for light, traveling at 186,000 miles per second, to be reflected on the retina of one's eye. In less than a nanosecond, the Lord will call believers to Himself!

THE RAPTURE IS A SELECTIVE EVENT

All three of the major passages that teach about the Rapture make it clear that it involves believers only (including innocent children too young to believe). In John 14:1-3, Jesus is speaking to His disciples who are obviously believers. His words, "I will come again and receive you to Myself" are what we call the Rapture—the uniting of Jesus Christ with His faithful followers.

In 1 Corinthians 15 Paul talks about "those *who are* Christ's at His coming" (verse 23). He concludes the passage by talking about their abounding in the work of the Lord (verse 58), an obvious reference to Christian believers.

Three times in 1 Thessalonians 4:13-18 he refers to believers as "brethren" (verse 13), as those who "believe that Jesus died and rose again" (verse 14), and as the "dead in Christ" (verse 16). The question is this: Were Jesus and Paul talking about you? Will you be a participant in the Rapture?

The Rapture Is a Spectacular Event

The actual Second Coming of Christ is described as a glorious event in Revelation 19:11-14, and rightly so. For that reason, the Rapture has traditionally played second fiddle to the Second Coming. But the Rapture itself will be a spectacular event.

One verse is all we need: "For the Lord Himself will descend from heaven with a shout, with the voice of an archangel, and with the trumpet of God" (1 Thessalonians 4:16). These are not three distinct sounds but one sound described three different ways.

This sound will be like a shout, ringing with commanding authority like the voice of an archangel. It will also be like the blare of a trumpet in its volume and clarity. And the sound will be heard only by those who have trusted Christ as Savior. Jesus shouted, "Lazarus, come forth!" in John 11:43. His shout of "Come forth!" at the Rapture will not name a single individual, but will be heard by every believer in every grave around the world.

Based purely on how the Rapture will sound—it will be a spectacular event.

The Rapture Is a Sequential Event

In 1 Thessalonians 4, Paul identifies five aspects of the Rapture in their sequential order.

The Return

The initiating event is Christ's return from heaven (verse 16). This fulfills the prophecy given by the angels the day Christ ascended into heaven—that the disciples would see Him return in like manner (Acts 1:11). Jesus ascended; Jesus will return. The same person who left earth will return.

The Resurrection

"The dead in Christ will rise first" (verse 16). "Sleep" is a biblical metaphor for death (John 11:11; Acts 7:60; 13:36). Those who have been "asleep" in Christ will be "awakened" and raised from the dead. How bodies dead for centuries, not to mention bodies that have been cremated or destroyed in explosions, will be recomposed and raised, we do not know. But they will be.

The Redemption

Following the resurrection of the dead, believers who are alive will rise to meet Christ in the air. They will experience the same physical transformation as the deceased, then resurrected, believers. Paul says in 1 Corinthians 15:51-52, "We shall not all sleep, but we shall all be changed—in a moment; in the twinkling of an eye, at the last trumpet." We will become like Christ's resurrected, glorified body, fit for heaven.

The Rapture and the Reunion

Translating living saints to heaven has happened before the Rapture. In fact, four raptures have already occurred. In the Old Testament; Enoch was taken to heaven without dying (Genesis 5:24), as was Elijah (2 Kings 2:1, 11). We have already mentioned Christ being taken up to heaven (Acts 1:11), and the apostle Paul also was taken up to "the third heaven" and returned to earth (2 Corinthians 12:2-4).

There are two raptures that are yet to occur. During the Tribulation, God's two witnesses will be taken to heaven while they are still living (Revelation 11:12). The primary Rapture yet to occur, of course, is the Rapture of the Church just before the beginning of the Tribulation.

There are three reunions, which will take place (verse 17).

First, dead bodies will reunite with their spirits which Christ will have brought with Him from heaven (verse 14). Deceased bodies will be reunited with their spirits.

Second, resurrected believers will meet living believers. It will be a reunion of saints from every era of history, uniting finally as the one, universal Church.

Third, together these groups will experience the joy of reunion with their Lord. They met Him first at their conversion, now they meet Him face to face.

THE RAPTURE IS A STRENGTHENING EVENT

The Rapture can change our life; it is a source of personal comfort and hope. The reason Paul wrote to the Thessalonians about it was to ease their concerns about their departed loved ones. Death is not final. The resurrection of believers who have died will reverse the effects of death. All who have lost loved ones to the sting of death can be comforted in the knowledge that they will see them again. But it is also a source of strength. Jesus promised His disciples, on the night He was arrested, that He would return for them (John 14:1-3).

It is no wonder that Paul told the Thessalonians to comfort themselves with the truth concerning the Rapture (1 Thessalonians 4:18). The Rapture can impact our life now, in three ways, while we wait for it to happen.

Expectation

The letter from Paul to Titus puts in words how the expectation of the Rapture should impact our life:

> For the grace of God that brings salvation has appeared to all men, teaching us that, denying ungodliness and worldly lusts, we should live soberly, righteously, and godly in the present age, looking for the blessed hope and glorious appearing of our great God and Savior Jesus Christ, who gave Himself for us, that He might redeem us from every lawless deed and purify for Himself His own special people, zealous for good works. (Titus 2:11-14)

Consecration

I am told that Robert Murray M'Cheyne, a brilliant young Scottish preacher who died at age 29 in 1843, wore a wristwatch with the words "The Night Cometh" engraved on its face. Every time he checked his watch he was reminded that time is marching on. We won't always have time to win souls to Christ and to consecrate our own lives for His service. The apostle John exhorted his readers to "not be ashamed before Him at His coming" (1 John 2:28). The any-moment imminent return of Jesus for His Church is life's greatest stimulus for living a consecrated life.

Examination

Jesus warned that He is "coming quickly" (Revelation 22:12). That means we should live every day as if He was coming that day. But will we be ready? Will we be found with heart and hands dedicated to serving Him at the moment we see Him face to face? Even more important have we committed ourselves by faith to Christ so we are assured of being part of His Church that is called into His presence at the Rapture? When the Rapture occurs, there will be no opportunity to make a decision. Be sure today that you have said yes to Christ so you will be prepared to rejoice at His appearing.

Notes

1. "The Second Coming of Christ" *preceptaustin.org.*, February 21, 2015, www.preceptaustin.org/the_second_coming_of_Christ.htm.
2. Chuck Swindoll, "Does the Bible Teach that Jesus Will Return?" *Jesus.org*, n.d., www.jesus.org/early-church-history/promise-of-the-second-coming/does-the-bible-teach-that-jesus-will-return.html.
3. Arthur T. Pierson, *Our Lord's Second Coming as a Motive to World-Wide Evangelism* (Published by John Wanamaker, n.d.). Quoted by Renald Showers in *Maranatha —Our Lord, Come!* (Bellmawr, NJ: The Friends of Israel Gospel Ministry, Inc., 1995), 127.

THE RAPTURE	THE RETURN (SECOND COMING)
Christ comes in the air (1 Thessalonians 4:16-17)	Christ comes to the earth (Zechariah 14:4)
Christ comes for His saints (1 Thessalonians 4:16-17)	Christ comes with His saints (1 Thessalonians 3:13; Jude 1:14)
Believers depart the earth (1 Thessalonians 4:16-17)	Unbelievers are taken away (Matthew 24:37-41)
Christ claims His bride	Christ comes with His bride
Christ gathers His own (1 Thessalonians 4:16-17)	Angels gather the elect (Matthew 24:31)
Christ comes to reward (1 Thessalonians 4:16-17)	Christ comes to judge (Matthew 25:31-46)
Not in the Old Testament (1 Corinthians 15:51)	Predicted often in the Old Testament
There are no signs. It is imminent.	Portended by many signs (Matthew 24:4-29)
It is a time of blessing and comfort (1 Thessalonians 4:17-18)	It is a time of destruction and judgment (2 Thessalonians 2:8-12)
Involves believers only (John 14:1-3; 1 Corinthians 15:51-55; 1 Thessalonians 4:13-18)	Involves Israel and the Gentile nations (Matthew 24:1-25:46)
Will occur in a moment, in the time it takes to blink. Only His own will see Him (1 Corinthians 15:51-52)	Will be visible to the entire world (Matthew 24:27; Revelation 1:7)
Tribulation begins	Millennium begins
Christ comes as the bright morning star (Revelation 22:16)	Christ comes as the Sun of Righteousness (Malachi 4:2)

Some content taken from *THE END*, by Mark Hitchcock. Copyright © 2012. Used by permission of Tyndale House Publishers, Inc. All rights reserved. www.tyndaledirect.com.

PERSONAL QUESTIONS

1. Which Scripture passages in the New Testament mention the Rapture?

    a. What do these passages teach about who will be raptured?

    b. What do these passages tell us about how Paul gained understanding about the Rapture?

    c. Why did Paul write to the Thessalonians about the Rapture?

d. How do Paul's words to the Thessalonians bring comfort and understanding to you?

2. Describe the differences between the Rapture and the Second Coming of Christ.

a. When does each event occur?

b. What is the purpose of each event?

3. Does the imminency of the Rapture impact how you live and how you interact with others?

   a. If so, how does it impact your life?

   b. If not, what changes do you need to make in your life in light of Christ's imminent return?

4. As you serve a Savior you've never seen, what does it mean to know you will one day be united with Him?

GROUP QUESTIONS

1. How would you summarize the Rapture?

2. Explain the four different meanings of the Greek word *harpazo* and how each definition relates to the Rapture.

3. Discuss the seven characteristics of the Rapture.

    a. Explain what is meant by the imminency of the Rapture?

    b. Who knows when the Rapture will occur?

c. How long will the Rapture take?

d. What will the sound that occurs at the Rapture be like? (see 1 Thessalonians 4:16)

4. What are the five aspects of the Rapture?

a. Discuss the four raptures that have already occurred.

b. What are the three reunions that will occur as part of the Rapture?

The Rapture of the Redeemed • 25

5. Share how the Rapture strengthens your faith.

   a. What hope does the Rapture give us?

   b. How does the imminency of the Rapture impact how we live here on earth?

DID YOU KNOW?

Have you ever thought about what people on earth will be experiencing in the moments after the Rapture? Dr. Tim LaHaye did. While he was traveling, he observed a flirtatious interaction between a married pilot and an unmarried flight attendant. He imagined the pilot's wife was a believing Christian and wondered what the pilot would do if some of his passengers were suddenly raptured. These thoughts sparked the *Left Behind* series, which Dr. LaHaye wrote with Jerry B. Jenkins. Their popular, fictional series about the Rapture and subsequent end-time events opened the eyes of many to the imminency of Christ's return and the reality of the End Times.[1]

1. Jerry B. Jenkins, "Jerry B. Jenkins, The Tim LaHaye I Knew," *Christianity Today*, July 25, 2016, https://www.christianitytoday.com/ct/2016/july-web-only/jerry-b-jenkins-tim-lahaye-i-knew-tribute-left-behind.html

LESSON 13

Resurrection
The Ultimate "Extreme Makeover"

1 Corinthians 15:35-49

In this lesson we discover the nature of the believer's resurrection body.

OUTLINE

Much speculation has been offered about what those who populate heaven will look like. Will they appear as angels? As "ghosts"? The Bible makes it clear that believers will have corporeal bodies that are recognizable, but which are free from all the limitations of bodies on planet earth.

I. The Requirement of Resurrection Is the Death of the Body

II. The Result of Resurrection Is a Different Kind of Body
   A. Our New Bodies Will Be Indestructible
   B. Our New Bodies Will Be Identifiable
   C. Our New Bodies Will Be Incredible
   D. Our New Bodies Will Be Infinite

OVERVIEW

As we begin this lesson on the Resurrection, here is an epitaph from Benjamin Franklin that ties in perfectly with the message of this lesson:

[Benjamin Franklin] . . . lies in the grave like the cover of an old book, with its contents torn out, stripped of its lettering, but which will appear once again in a new and more eloquent edition, revised and corrected by the author.[1]

Those words eloquently describe the ultimate "extreme makeover" every Christian will one day receive from God. In 1 Corinthians 15, Paul deals with the doctrine of the resurrection—both the resurrection of Christ and of the believer. As part of that doctrine, he talks about the change that will occur in our physical bodies when we are resurrected at the end of this age.

THE REQUIREMENT OF RESURRECTION IS THE DEATH OF THE BODY

There is a prerequisite for having a resurrection body: First you have to have a dead body! I think Paul is having a little fun with the Corinthians when he says, "Foolish one, what you sow is not made alive unless it dies" (verse 36).

Here Paul is obviously picking up on the teaching of Jesus who said in John 12:24, "Most assuredly, I say to you, unless a grain of wheat falls into the ground and dies, it remains alone; but if it dies, it produces much grain."

The biblical perspective on death is different from the world's. Death is to be embraced, not feared. Death is the precursor to the wonderful resurrection body God has planned for the believer. If we did not die, we would be stuck with our current body for all eternity. Paul strikes a positive note right up front, saying that death is not to be feared. It's what has to occur before we can be changed. Without death there is no resurrection.

THE RESULT OF RESURRECTION IS A DIFFERENT KIND OF BODY

In the next two verses, Paul makes an important point: The seed is one thing, the body of the plant it produces is another. In other words, sow one shape or form and reap another—a kernel of corn is radically different from the tall, green stalk that emerges from the earth. Applied to the human body, the body that dies and is buried in the earth is raised as a totally different kind of body. On the day of our resurrection, the body that comes out of the ground will be very different from the body that went into the ground.

Paul gives us four ways in which the bodies that come out of the ground will be different from the bodies that were buried in the ground.

Our New Bodies Will Be Indestructible

There has only been one body that was perfect—incorruptible —and that was the body of Jesus Christ. This was prophesied by the psalmist who wrote, "nor will You allow Your Holy One to see corruption" (Psalm 16:10). Our bodies, however, are "sown [buried] in corruption."

Our present bodies get old, wear out, and eventually die. Things stop working like they once did, all part of the aging process of "corruptible" bodies. Despite the claims of science, there is nothing that will ever grant us immortality on this earth. On the other hand, our resurrected bodies will be incorruptible—they will last forever! They will not age, wear out, or be susceptible to disease.

I ride a bike now for exercise, and I have learned that it is much easier to go with the wind than against it. But that won't be true in heaven because my resurrection body will not get tired, strained, or become short of breath. Our bodies will be perfect in every way— indestructible!

Our New Bodies Will Be Identifiable

Second, we are not going to be ghost-like apparitions that all look the same. Our new bodies will be identifiable. Paul says our new bodies will be "raised in glory," which literally means "brilliance."

I don't know if we're going to have a brilliant "glow" or not. We have to look at Philippians 3:20-21 to get an idea of what Paul is probably talking about here. There Paul says that our "lowly body" will be conformed to Christ's "glorious body." Our new bodies will be like the body of the Lord Jesus Christ. The apostle John wrote that "it has not yet been revealed what we shall be, but we know that when He is revealed, we shall be like Him, for we shall see Him as He is" (1 John 3:2). Paul concludes this thought in verse 4 of 1 Corinthians 15 by saying, "And as we have borne the image of the man of dust [Adam], we shall also bear the image of the heavenly Man [Christ]."

The best glimpse we have of what Jesus' glorified body was like (and thus what our resurrected bodies will be like) is in the forty-day period between His resurrection and ascension. We can identify four characteristics of His body during that period:

1. Jesus Said That His Body Was Real (Luke 24:39)

   Jesus, when He met with the disciples after His resurrection, invited them to touch Him to see that His body was real: "Handle Me and see, for a spirit does not have flesh and bones as you see I have." Jesus had a physical, corporeal body after His resurrection from the dead.

2. Jesus Ate on at Least Two Occasions (Luke 24:42-43; John 21:12-13)

   People ask me this question about heaven more than any other: "Are we going to eat in heaven?" Apparently so, since Jesus ate in His post-resurrection body. He ate a piece of fish and some honeycomb on one occasion (Luke 24), and (apparently) shared fish and bread with His disciples on the shores of the Sea of Galilee (John 21).

   It seems that the role of food changes from being a necessity to a pleasure. We won't need to eat to stay alive because our bodies will be incorruptible. But we will enjoy the pleasure of eating just as Adam and Eve would have done in the Garden of Eden before they sinned.

3. Jesus Told Thomas to Touch His Body (John 20:27)

   When Thomas doubted that Jesus had really been raised from the dead, Jesus encouraged him to reach out and touch His wounds, to see that it was really Jesus in the body in which He had been crucified.

4. Jesus Told Mary Not to Hold on to Him (John 20:17)

When Mary encountered Jesus in the garden after His resurrection, He cautioned her not to cling to Him—to throw her arms around Him. He would not have said that had it not been possible for her to cling to Him; that is, if His body had not been a true physical body.

So, if our bodies are going to be like Jesus' body, we will be physical, we will be recognizable, we will be able to eat, and we'll be able to communicate. Jesus was as recognizable and communicable after His resurrection as He was before His death. Paul says in 1 Corinthians 13:12, "Now I know in part, but then I shall know just as I also am known." In heaven, we will know and be known.

On the Mount of Transfiguration, Moses and Elijah were recognized by the disciples (Matthew 17:1-4), and Jesus said that in the kingdom "many will come from east and west, and sit down with Abraham, Isaac, and Jacob in the kingdom of heaven" (Matthew 8:11). It would be hard to sit down with Abraham if you couldn't tell who he was!

Our New Bodies Will Be Incredible

Paul says our bodies are sown in weakness (death is the ultimate weakness), but "raised in power." When we come out of the grave, we will come out as power personified. The weakness we experience now will be a thing of our past life.

When a group from our church went to Africa on a missions trip, we experienced just what physical weakness is all about. Our task was to work in the vegetable gardens that were being planted as a source of food for African villagers. We went out strong in the morning; but when we returned in the evening, we looked bad—like we'd been run over by a truck! The work was hard; and as the week wore on, our stamina decreased markedly. In this life we simply do not have the power we need to do all we would like to do.

On one occasion after His resurrection, Jesus just appeared in a room where the disciples were. He didn't use the door—He was just there (John 20:19). Will we have that same kind of power in our resurrected bodies—the ability to transport ourselves from one place to another? To the degree that we are like Jesus in His resurrected body, I would think so, though we can't know for sure.

The point is that we can't even imagine what it will be like to live in bodies that are not limited as our current physical bodies are. Jesus was not constrained by the limitations of His earthly body, and neither will we be in the resurrection.

Our New Bodies Will Be Infinite

Finally, Paul draws a distinction between a natural body and a spiritual one. In this passage, he points to Adam as the image bearer for our natural body and to Christ, the last Adam, as the image bearer for the spiritual body we will receive.

What is a "spiritual" body? First, Paul doesn't mean it is an immaterial body. We've already seen that Jesus had a physical body, and so will we—a body that can be touched and felt. Instead, a spiritual body is one that is not controlled by the physical appetites of the fallen, carnal human nature. Instead, our bodies will be spiritual, controlled by the Holy Spirit. The basic difference between natural bodies and spiritual bodies is that one is at home on the earth, and the other is at home in heaven. That's why Paul says our natural bodies cannot inherit the kingdom of God (1 Corinthians 15:50).

Our current bodies are completely unsuited for heaven, which is why God will give us new ones when we are resurrected from the dead. Our spiritual bodies will welcome the control of the Spirit, and we will no longer have to contend with the flesh. If you have ever had a brief period of time, even just a few moments, where you felt completely in step with the Spirit of God, you have tasted heaven. It will be a time when our desires and the desires of God are one. There will be no conflict, no competition between Spirit and flesh. Our whole desire will be to do the will of God. Watch for those moments in this life and, when they happen, remind yourself that you are headed for an eternity of such bliss if you know Jesus as your Savior.

So Paul summarizes the order of events in verses 51 and 52: Some will be alive when Christ comes, and some will be "asleep," having already died. But all will be changed in a moment of time when the last trumpet sounds and the dead are raised and changed from corruption into incorruption.

From 1 Thessalonians 4, we can add the specific order of the changes that will take place. The dead in Christ will rise first; then those who are alive when Christ returns will join them in the air, and all will be changed. Instantaneously—"in the twinkling of an eye" (1 Corinthians 15:52)—our corruptible, natural, weak, and limited bodies will become incorruptible, spiritual, powerful, and limitless bodies.

I sincerely hope I am alive when that happens—when Christ returns for His Church at the Rapture. I believe we ought to all have that longing and hope, to hear the trumpet and the archangel's shout, to see our Savior in the clouds, and to experience the transformation of our bodies. What a glorious moment to live for!

What a blessed hope we have, to know that whether we are alive or not when He comes, we shall all be changed!

Joni Eareckson Tada is one of many saints who have experienced physical disabilities and limitations in this life, and she has written beautifully about her hope and God's promise for a new body:

> I still can hardly believe it. I, with shriveled, bent fingers, atrophied muscles, gnarled knees, and no feeling from the shoulders down, will one day have a new body, light, bright,

and clothed in righteousness—powerful and dazzling. Can you imagine the hope this gives someone spinal-cord injured like me? Or someone who is cerebral palsied, brain-injured, or who has multiple sclerosis? Imagine the hope this gives someone who is manic-depressive. No other religion, no other philosophy promises new bodies, hearts, and minds. Only in the Gospel of Christ do hurting people find such incredible hope.[2]

No wonder Paul said that if in this life only we have hope, we are most miserable (1 Corinthians 15:19, KJV). But we have hope beyond this life. And that hope is in Jesus. One day all of the pains and the aches and the deformities and the deficiencies that we carry in our earthly bodies are going to be taken away when we get our heavenly bodies. We will know the joy of living in the perfection and glory that God intended for us from the beginning.

This truth about our new physical bodies is not the least of the reasons I am passionate about taking people to heaven with me. I don't want anyone to miss what God has planned for those who are His.

The reality of a new body is part of the expectation of glory that heaven represents. Since we have never lived in perfect, limitless, spiritual bodies, it's very difficult to imagine what it will be like. The surest way to find out is to experience the change yourself by being one of those Christ calls to Himself when He comes for His own. Make sure you have entrusted yourself to Him by faith and that you enter eternity with your ultimate "extreme makeover"!

Notes

1. http://sln.fi.edu/franklin/timeline/epitaph.html.
2. Joni Eareckson Tada, *Heaven: Your Real Home* (Grand Rapids: Zondervan, 1955), 53.

PERSONAL QUESTIONS

1. Turn to 1 Corinthians 15:36-43.

    a. What must happen to believers before being resurrected? (verse 36; see also John 12:24)

    b. According to Paul, the body is sown in_____ and raised in_____. (verse 42)

    c. Is there anything on earth that will grant you immortality? Only where will you have eternal life?

    d. We will be buried in dishonor and weakness, but raised in what? (see verse 43)

2. What reason do you have, as a follower of Christ, not to be afraid of death?

   a. Paul says death will be swallowed up in what? (1 Corinthians 15:54)

   b. How quickly will believers be changed when Christ returns for His Church? (verse 52)

3. Read John 20:16-17, 24-28.

   a. What is the implication of Jesus' words to Mary concerning the nature of His resurrected body? (verse 17) (Is it possible to "cling to" a spirit?)

b. What physical evidence did Jesus offer Thomas of His resurrection? (verse 27)

4. In what should you have hope, if not in your life on earth? (see 1 Corinthians 15:19-20)

   a. What assurance do you have that you will be granted a heavenly body? (verse 20, NIV)

GROUP QUESTIONS

1. Read 2 Corinthians 5:1-10.

   a. What metaphor does Paul use to describe our earthly body? (verse 1)

   b. What is waiting for us when our earthly sojourn is finished? (verse 1)

   c. What is implied in verse 2 concerning the difference between earthly life and heavenly life?

   d. What is the meaning of verse 3 concerning our heavenly existence? Will we be "spirits" or corporeal bodies in heaven?

e. How did Paul reverse that image in verse 4?

f. Who did the Old Testament saints see doing the "swallowing" in this life? (verse 4; see Psalm 69:15; Proverbs 1:12)

g. What guarantee have we been given that death is going to be "swallowed up by life"? (verse 5; see Ephesians 1:13)

h. What tension do Christians live with while on earth? (verse 6)

i. Since we have never seen heaven or our new heavenly bodies, what should be the basis of our hope? (verse 7)

j. Given a choice, where would Paul rather be? (verse 8)

k. In either place, what should be our highest priority as Christians? (verse 9)

l. What motivates our desire to be well-pleasing to the Lord? (verse 10; see also 1 Corinthians 3:11-15)

The Ultimate "Extreme Makeover" • 39

DID YOU KNOW?

Several resurrections from the dead were recorded in the New Testament. Jesus raised the deceased son of a widow from the dead (Luke 7:11-15), as well as His friend Lazarus (John 11:38-44). He also brought the daughter of Jairus, a synagogue ruler, back to life (Mark 5:22-24). The apostle Peter raised a young man named Eutychus from the dead in Troas (Acts 20:7-12). The bodies of those raised from the dead were not, however, "resurrection bodies"—mortality putting on immortality (1 Corinthians 15:53-54). Each of those raised from the dead died a second time later in their lives to await their immortal resurrection.

LESSON 14

Heaven
What's Up With Heaven?

Selected Scriptures

In this lesson we learn why heaven is such an important place for the Christian.

OUTLINE

Everyone has heard the expression, "Oh, this is just heaven!" Granted, it's a figure of speech, but it betrays the casual approach most people take to something that is biblically serious. Since heaven is the eternal home of Christians, we should know all there is to know about it.

I. **The Prominence of Heaven**

II. **The Plurality of Heaven**
  A. The First Heaven
  B. The Second Heaven
  C. The Third Heaven

III. **The Place Called Heaven**

IV. **The Preciousness of Heaven**
  A. Our Redeemer Is in Heaven
  B. Our Relationships Are in Heaven
  C. Our Resources Are in Heaven
  D. Our Residence Is in Heaven
  E. Our Reward Is in Heaven
  F. Our Riches Are in Heaven
  G. Our Reservation Is in Heaven

OVERVIEW

When a Sunday school teacher quizzed her class of fifth-graders about how one gets to heaven, she got all correct answers: One doesn't get there by being good, giving away money, or being a nice person. "Well, then," she asked, "how does one get to heaven?" Before any of the regular students could answer, a boy who was visiting the class that week shouted out, "You have to be dead!"

That's the correct answer, isn't it? Unless Jesus Christ returns and takes us off the earth to be with Him in heaven, we have to die to get there. Worldwide, nearly 2 people die every second. That means more than 6,000 people every hour are passing from life to death and going either to heaven or to hell—more than 151,000 people every day.[1]

A 2003 Harris Poll found that 82 percent of Americans believe in heaven and 63 percent said they expected to go there when they die. In spite of all that interest in heaven, there is little talk about heaven in American churches whether evangelical, mainline Protestant, or Catholic.[2]

Other polls from the Barna and Gallup organizations tell us there is little difference between the morals and lifestyles of Christians and non-Christians. And I believe the absence of a focus on heaven is in large part to blame. When we lose sight of the fact that God has a wonderful destination prepared for those who are His, we start trying to create heaven on earth. We start investing our time and talent and treasure in creating a place that we know in our heart is what we were created for (Ecclesiastes 3:11). We know there is supposed to be a heaven; and when we stop seeking the biblical heaven, we try to create an earthly one.

The problem with that strategy is that we could never approximate on earth what God has created for us in heaven—so we try harder. And we begin pursuing the pleasures of this world. We begin doing what Solomon writes about in Ecclesiastes, looking for pleasure and satisfaction in wine, women, and wealth. He finally recognized the futility (vanity) of his ways, but many Christians have not. If we do not feed the hunger for heaven with biblical truth, we will feed it the superficial baubles and bangles of this world.

THE PROMINENCE OF HEAVEN

While heaven isn't being talked about much in churches, it seems to be popping up in the popular culture. A book called *The*

Five People You Meet in Heaven, by Mitch Albom, was on *The New York Times* bestseller list for more than a year—but it has nothing to do with heaven. It has to do with evaluating how you treated people on earth when you meet them in heaven. The famous *Left Behind* series has sold millions of books and deals a lot with heaven. And a book called *Heaven* by an evangelical author, Randy Alcorn, was published in 2004 and sold a hundred thousand copies in just a few months. So people are reading about heaven—we're just not talking about it in church very much.

Heaven is mentioned more than five hundred times in Scripture. Both the Old Testament (*shamayim*) and the New Testament (*ouranos*) words for heaven refer to high and lofty places. Heaven is a consistent theme in the Bible. It is discussed in our culture, but the average Christian knows little about it.

THE PLURALITY OF HEAVEN

The Bible speaks of three heavens. Paul, when writing to the Corinthian believers, talks about being "caught up to the third heaven" (2 Corinthians 12:2), a place he then refers to as "Paradise" (verse 4). We have to conclude that if Paul visited the third heaven, there must be a first and second heaven as well.

The First Heaven

We could call this heaven the "atmospheric" heaven—a place mentioned numerous times in Scripture: "For as the heavens are higher than the earth.... For as the rain comes down ... from heaven" (Isaiah 55:9-10). This heaven is the atmosphere surrounding the earth—the domain of clouds and birds (Genesis 1:20).

The Second Heaven

This heaven is mentioned early in the book of Genesis and is the domain of the heavenly bodies: the sun, moon, stars, planets, and galaxies besides our own. We refer to this today as "outer space" where satellites and planetary space probes travel.

The Third Heaven

When Paul described being caught up to the third heaven [II Corinthians], he didn't say where it was. In fact, he seemed not to know: "Whether in the body I do not know, or whether out of the body I do not know." We can only assume it was a place beyond the atmospheric and stellar heavens—the dwelling place of God.

Jesus taught His disciples to pray, "Our Father in heaven ..." (Matthew 6:9), and referred in Matthew 5:16 to "Your Father in heaven." Psalm 11:4 says, "The Lord's throne is in heaven." That must be the heaven to which Paul was taken by God—either physically or spiritually—the heaven where God dwells. This is the heaven that is our destination as believers in Christ.

The Place Called Heaven

John 14 is a classic text on the subject of heaven where we learn from Jesus Christ Himself as He raised the subject with His disciples.

The disciples of Christ were greatly troubled at the timeline that had been laid out for them concerning Jesus' future: He would die, be buried, be resurrected, and then return to heaven. Not understanding the complete picture of Christ's mission, they were understandably sorrowful at this news that He was going to leave them. But in John 14:1-4, He gives them a truth to comfort them in their sorrows: "I'm going to prepare a place for you in My Father's house so that you can one day join Me there forever" (paraphrase).

Then Jesus replied to Thomas's doubts (verse 5) by saying, "No one comes to the Father except through Me" (verse 6). That is, not just His disciples would be joining Him in heaven, but all who believed in Him. Heaven is a real place being prepared by Christ to receive all those who belong to Him. Jesus didn't leave His disciples or us to find heaven on earth. He went to prepare heaven for us.

While heaven is referred to in Jesus' parables by many metaphors (country, city, kingdom), the picture I like best is the one here in John 14: the Father's house. Those who grew up in a warm and loving house know it as a place you long to return to. When we were younger, my wife and I would drive two thousand miles round trip over a weekend just to spend a few hours in "the father's house." When my dad eventually became a widower and sold his home, I hated to see us lose it because of what it represented: the place to which we could always return.

Fortunately, we don't have to worry about losing our heavenly Father's house since Christ has gone to heaven to prepare it for us. It is a permanent, heavenly abode where we will dwell forever in God's presence. Heaven is not a feeling or an emotion or a point of view or an attitude. It is not a place we create by our actions here on earth. It is a "place" (Greek *topos*, in John 14:2; a physical, locatable place).

Where, exactly, is the place called heaven? We can't say with certainty because the Bible doesn't say. But Ephesians 4:10 says it is above all the heavens, where Christ ascended; and in Acts 1:10-11, the disciples were gazing "up into heaven" where Jesus had gone. If language means anything, we have to assume that Jesus' destination was "up."

But depending upon where you are standing on earth, "up" is a different direction—it just means perpendicular to the surface of the planet. But in Isaiah 14, we get a different perspective. Addressing God, Satan says, "I will exalt my throne above the stars of God; I will also sit on the mount of the congregation on the farthest sides of the north" (verse 13). Satan refers to heaven as the "farthest sides of the north." Regardless of where you are on the globe, north is always pointing in the same direction. So it may be reasonable to conclude that heaven is somewhere in the northern heavens beyond the range of the astronomers' most powerful telescopes. Astronomers even tell us that this part of outer space contains fewer stars and galaxies than other parts.

So, even if we don't know exactly where the third heaven is, we know it's a specific place where Jesus is preparing a place for us.

The Preciousness of Heaven

Everything that should be precious to a follower of Christ applies to heaven because that's where Christ is, where He will be forever, and where we will be with Him. Here are seven reasons why heaven is a precious place.

Our Redeemer Is in Heaven

Hebrews 9:24 says Christ has entered "into heaven itself, now to appear in the presence of God for us." The descriptions of heaven in Revelation suggest it is going to be a stunningly beautiful place, but I believe all that beauty will pale into insignificance when we behold the beauty of our Redeemer, Jesus Christ. When we see the One who suffered and died to pay the penalty for our sins . . . when we see the scars of His suffering, I think nothing will look as beautiful as He will look to our eyes when we see Him as He really is.

Our Relationships Are in Heaven

My father told me as he grew old and began to see his friends pass away, "One of the hard things about getting old is you have more friends in heaven than you do on earth." That's true, but what a wonderful truth! My wife and I have lost all four of our parents, but we know where they are—they are in heaven. And we rejoice that one day we will be reunited with them.

The writer to the Hebrews made an interesting choice of words when he wrote, "To the general assembly and church of the firstborn who are registered in heaven" (12:23). It sounds like checking in at a hotel, doesn't it? You leave earth and arrive in heaven and are registered there. So when we get there, we will look up our friends and loved ones and be reunited for all eternity.

Our Resources Are in Heaven

First Peter 1:3-4 says that our inheritance is "reserved in heaven." When you became a Christian, God became your Father. And when God is your Father, you are one of His heirs, which means you have an inheritance waiting for you in heaven. Peter says that inheritance has preceded us to heaven—it is already there waiting for us to arrive and claim it. Unlike earthly inheritances, our heavenly inheritance is not dependent on the economy as to its value. It has been perfectly established in heaven and will never change.

Our Residence Is in Heaven

Philippians 3:20 says that "our citizenship is in heaven." We are not citizens of earth who are going to heaven; we are citizens of heaven who are traveling through earth. When we fill out paperwork in this life, we have to declare our place of birth and our residence—but that's all just temporary. My real residence is in heaven, and I'm currently here as an ambassador.

Our Reward Is in Heaven

Jesus told His disciples to "Rejoice and be exceedingly glad, for great *is* your reward in heaven" (Matthew 5:12). We will spend an entire lesson in this series on the rewards of heaven in lesson 16. As a preview, we can note here that there are five crowns that can be earned by Christians on earth, crowns which will be awarded in heaven.

Some think it is not very spiritual to be looking forward to heaven in order to receive a reward. But God is big on rewards! All throughout Scripture, God makes promises that have positive benefits as their rewards. God motivates us to faithfulness by offering rewards. That is perfectly reasonable since our fallen human nature is not inclined to be faithful or obedient. So God motivates us to be faithful and then rewards us when we are. It's a great program!

Amazingly, we will end up casting all those crowns and rewards at the feet of Jesus in honor and praise of Him (Revelation 4:10; more on this in an upcoming lesson).

Our Riches Are in Heaven

Another reason why heaven is so precious is that our riches are in heaven. In Matthew 6:19-21, Jesus tells His followers not to lay up treasures on earth, but to lay them up in heaven where they would be eternally safe: "For where your treasure is, there your heart will be also" (verse 21).

How do we store up treasure in heaven? By investing on earth in the only things that are going to be transferred to heaven, and that is the souls of men and women and boys and girls. The Word of God and the human soul are the only eternal things on earth. So to build equity in heaven, we have to build the Word of God into the lives of people on earth.

Our Reservation Is in Heaven

Revelation 21:27 says that "only those who are written in the Lamb's Book of Life" will be allowed into heaven. If you belong to Christ, then your name is recorded in that book in heaven. Jesus once told His disciples to rejoice that their names were "written in heaven" (Luke 10:20)—and we should likewise rejoice.

As we study the end-time events that are all around us, it's the right time for you to confirm that your name is written in the Lamb's Book of Life. If you have never asked God to forgive your sins through Christ's death in your place on the cross, do so now. Heaven is not a place you want to miss!

Notes

1. "World Birth and Death Rates," *Ecology*, 2011, www.ecology.com/birth-death-rates/.
2. Cary McMullen, "Heaven: A Lot of Questions, But No One Really Knows the Answers," *The Ledger*, March 27, 2005.

PERSONAL QUESTIONS

1. Read 2 Corinthians 12:2-4.

    a. Where was the apostle Paul "caught up"? (verse 2)

    b. Where did he say that place was located (verse 3), and what did he refer to that place as? (verse 4)

2. Turn to John 14:1-4 in your Bible.

    a. What did Christ tell His disciples in verse 1? For what reason did He say this? Does this verse give you comfort today?

    b. Where did Christ go to prepare a place for believers? (verse 2)

    c. What did Christ promise to believers in verse 3?

3. According to Matthew 5:12, what did Jesus tell His disciples would be waiting for them in heaven?

   a. Jesus told His followers to do what in Matthew 6:19-21?

   b. Are there any "treasures" you are storing up on earth? What can you do to avoid this habit?

4. Read Revelation 21:27.

   a. Where will the names of those who are saved be written?

   b. Have you asked God to forgive your sins through Christ's death on the cross? If not, think about praying that prayer today so that you do not miss out on the place He is preparing for you.

What's Up With Heaven?

GROUP QUESTIONS

1. What does the plural "heavens" in Genesis 1:1 suggest about how many heavens there are?

   a. Which heaven did the apostle Paul visit? (2 Corinthians 12:2)

   b. If there is a "third heaven," at least how many divisions of heaven must there be?

   c. What characterizes the layer of heaven that is nearest to earth? (Genesis 7:11; Psalm 78:23; Daniel 7:13)

   d. What characterizes the next highest level of heaven? (Genesis 1:14-19; Psalm 19:4-6)

e. What other word did Paul use to describe the "third heaven"? (2 Corinthians 12:4)

f. What do you learn about this part of heaven from Revelation 2:7?

g. Though 2 Corinthians 5:8 doesn't use the word heaven, how is it consistent with Luke 23:43?

2. Discuss the details about heaven that you can discover from John 14:1-4:

   a. What Jesus called it (verse 2):

   b. Why Jesus was going there (verse 2):

What's Up With Heaven? • 51

c. Who the future occupants will be (verse 3):

   d. What level of comfort the anticipation of heaven should provide (verse 1):

3. If comfortable doing so, share with your group about a friend or family member who has yet to accept the gift of salvation. If time allows for it, pray for those mentioned that they might come to Christ.

DID YOU KNOW?

An obscure reference to the "queen of heaven" occurs five times in the book of Jeremiah (7:18; 44:17, 18, 19, 25). The "queen" is not named but was undoubtedly a female goddess in the pagan pantheon of the day (possibly Ishtar, a female Babylonian deity). Jeremiah 7:18 mentions the involvement of the whole family in worshiping the "queen of heaven": "The children gather wood, the fathers kindle the fire, and the women knead dough, to make cakes for the queen of heaven." In addition to making cakes, the Israelites burned incense and poured out drink offerings to this pagan deity (44:18, 19). Heaven and its occupants were a focus of speculation among ancient peoples—and even Israelites who had rejected the God of heaven.

LESSON 15

Judgment Seat of Christ
The Pretenders

Selected Scriptures

In this lesson we learn about the judgment that followers of Christ will face one day.

OUTLINE

Almost everyone has at least a vague concept about a future judgment where everyone will stand before God. But few Christians realize that the Bible teaches there will be not just one, but two different days of judgment! And it will be our relationship with Christ that will ultimately determine which judgment we will face.

I. **The Great White Throne Judgment**

II. **Judgment Seat of Christ**

III. **The Judge**

IV. **The Judged**

V. **The Judgment**
   A. The Confusion About This Judgment
   B. The Chronology of This Judgment
   C. The Courtroom of This Judgment
   D. The Criteria for This Judgment
   E. The Conclusion of This Judgment

OVERVIEW

It would be hard to ignore the fact that there is a lot of pretending going on in the world today. People pretend to be wealthier or stronger or happier or thinner than what reality testifies to be true. It is also popular to pretend to be spiritual, and some even pretend to be Christians, even though they are acutely aware that there has never been a life-changing experience of salvation in their lives.

But Christians like to play that game, too! We pretend to really love the Lord and be in fellowship with Him. We even go through the motions of serving Him, when in fact our hearts are far from that place—and we know it. So what is to become of all this pretending by us, the pretenders?

The Bible says that one day, all role-playing will finally be unmasked. All pretense will be exposed. God's Word assures us that a final judgment is coming—there is no denying that reality. Hebrews 9:27 says, "And as it is appointed for men to die once, but after this the judgment." There will actually be two judgments in the time to come, and they are very different from one another. Let's quickly look at each one.

THE GREAT WHITE THRONE JUDGMENT

Let's first take a look at the second judgment: the Great White Throne Judgment. At this time all unbelievers and those who pretended to be Christians will stand before God (Revelation 20:5, 11-15). There they will face the consequences of rejecting Jesus Christ as their Savior and Lord. This is the final judgment in God's justice plan for the inhabitants of planet Earth. There will be no grading on a curve, and the accused will be judged by the black-and-white standard of absolute truth and justice.

The Great White Throne Judgment is the final sentence for those who have rejected Christ—they will face an eternity without God. By the grace of God, I pray that you will not be one of those present for that judgment. Your goal in life should be to make certain that you have chosen the right path and to avoid being present at the Great White Throne. You don't want to be there, because if you are, it is too late. There is no plan for you to have a second chance after that.

Judgment Seat of Christ

But there is a judgment before that reserved just for Christians. This first judgment—the Judgment Seat of Christ—will happen one thousand years before the Great White Throne Judgment. It occurs right after the Rapture of the Church. Second Corinthians 5:10 describes it: "For we must all appear before the judgment seat of Christ, that each one may receive the things done in the body, according to what he has done, whether good or bad."

Please note that the purpose of this judgment is not to pronounce condemnation. No one judged at this court will be condemned. All who are present at this court will already be followers of Christ. They will just have been raised in their resurrection bodies to stand at the Judgment Seat as believers before the God of heaven. The purpose of this first judgment is for Christ to assess every believer's earthly works to determine what rewards are to be received.

The expression "judgment seat" is the translation of one little Greek word: *bema*. And the word *bema* is an interesting term because it means a "raised platform." According to one historian, "In Grecian games in Athens, the old arena contained a raised platform to which the president or umpire of the arena sat. From here he rewarded all the contestants; and here he rewarded all winners. It was called the 'bema' or 'reward seat.'"

From this exalted platform, the judges of the Greek Olympic games reviewed the preparation, training, and performance of each of the contestants and rewarded the winners who had kept the rules. They would be there for more than a week as the participants would come and go through all of the competitions. And the athletes would be judged not just as to whether or not they won the competition, but if they had participated according to the rules that had been set down for the competition itself.

So when Paul speaks of the Judgment Seat of Christ, the "bema seat," he is referring to the future judgment of Christians. This is not a judicial, courtroom-like event. Instead, the picture painted here is of an athletic event where the participants are being rewarded by a judge who is elevated up on a high platform, viewing everything from a broad perspective.

In this study, we are going to examine what Scripture says about the Judgment Seat of Christ. We will look at it from three perspectives. First, we will explore the Judge. Secondly, we will determine who the judged are. And finally, we will look at the judgment itself.

The Pretenders • 55

The Judge

The God of the Bible is a God who makes judgments. This first occurred in the Garden of Eden when Adam and Eve were judged for their disobedience. Judgment is a thread that runs through the whole Bible—from Genesis 3 to Revelation 22. According to Hebrews 4:13, "there is no creature hidden from His sight, but all things are naked and open to the eyes of Him to whom we must give account." The whole universe is subject to the dictates of the Judge.

On the awesome day of reckoning at the Judgment Seat, only God is qualified to make the judgment. And John 5:22, 27 tells us that God "has committed all judgment to the Son . . . and has given Him authority to execute judgment." Moreover, Acts 10:42 says that Jesus Christ "was ordained by God to be Judge of the living and the dead."

When you stand before the Judgment Seat of Christ, it won't be a judgment based on a group of your peers. Your wife or your husband won't be there to bring judgment against you, nor will your children or grandchildren. That judgment will be pronounced, presided over, and made by the Judge of all the earth, the Lord God of heaven, Jesus Christ. There is nothing that escapes His omniscient wisdom. He sees it all.

The Judged

Next we need to determine who exactly are the judged that come before this Judgment Seat of Christ. If you only take away one thing from this study, let it be this point: The Judgment Seat of Christ is for believers only. No unbelievers will be present at the Judgment Seat of Christ. At this tribunal, everyone who has accepted Jesus as their personal Savior will give a personal account of themselves before the Lord. No unsaved person will appear there. The Judgment Seat of Christ is for believers only.

There are three sections of Scripture in the New Testament that give us everything that we know about the Judgment Seat: Romans 14:10-12; 2 Corinthians 5:10; 1 Corinthians 3:11-15.

In all of these passages, it is important to note that all the pronouns are personal and singular. In other words, this event is not a community affair. This is not a church gathering. This judgment is a one-on-one interview with the Son of the Living God, and each of us will have our own personal appointment.

The Judgment

I am often asked about specific details about this important event in the life of a Christian. In this section, we will review five specific areas that correlate to this event. First, let's dispel some of the misconceptions about the Judgment Seat of Christ.

The Confusion About This Judgment

There are many false ideas that have emerged about the meaning of the Judgment Seat of Christ. We don't have time to go through all of them, but I do want to scrutinize the two most commonly conveyed errors.

The first faulty idea is that the judgment that takes place at the time of death is to determine whether a person is permitted to enter heaven or not. This is the oft-portrayed picture of standing at heaven's gate where God takes all of our good works and He weighs them against our bad deeds. And based upon which side prevails, we get to go to heaven or we're kept out.

Here is some good news for you: That is not what happens. There is no such event in the future. And we should all be so grateful that such a scenario does not exist, because each and every one of us would fail such a judgment.

The truth is that the only judgment a believer in Jesus Christ will ever be subjected to is the judgment of the Cross.[2] We were judged when Jesus died on the cross. We were in Christ on the cross when the Father poured out His wrath upon Him for sin. The sin was not His, but ours. And Jesus took all of our punishment for us. When He was judged for our sin, our sin was forever and finally judged.

So if you have confessed and accepted Jesus as Lord, you will never again face the judgment for your sin from God. That judgment is past—it's history. You don't see it through the front window; you see it through the rearview mirror. It has already happened.

The second faulty idea sometimes put forth is that the Judgment Seat of Christ is a judgment of all sins that a believer commits after they become a believer. The gross error conveyed here is that the Cross takes care of all your sins up to the point of salvation. But after that, you're on your own.

Nothing could be further from the truth. Just consider Romans 8:1, "There is therefore now no condemnation to those who are in Christ Jesus." It is ridiculous to think that somehow the salvation of a Christian is made up of everything Jesus did for you before you believed in Him. And then after you believed in Him, you have to do everything for yourself. Nonsense!

When Jesus died on the cross, how many of your sins were still in the future? All of them! So when Jesus died on the cross, what happened there was sufficient for all the sin that we would ever commit from that moment on—forevermore. Your sins have been forgiven. God has paid for all those sins through the sacrifice of His Son, Jesus Christ.

If we take our stand by the Cross, we are safe for time and eternity. The judgment has fallen, and it can never get to us again. The cross of Jesus Christ has scorched the earth for all future judgment. We will never face our sin in terms of judgment again.

The Chronology of This Judgment

So when does this all take place? The Judgment Seat of Christ is an event that is going to occur as soon as you get to heaven. As soon as you go through the pearly gates, the first agenda item will be to get your appointment with the Judge.

Revelation 22:12 says, "And behold, I am coming quickly, and My reward is with Me, to give to every one according to his work." The Bible pictures Jesus coming back to get us, bringing the rewards with Him so that as soon as we get back to heaven, He can give us our rewards at the Judgment Seat of Christ.

The Courtroom of This Judgment

The next natural question to ask is: Where will this all take place? Well, we've already indirectly discussed that question—it will be in heaven. So obviously whether we go to heaven or not isn't the issue—all believers will be there. You can't be at the Judgment Seat of Christ if you're not already in heaven. The Judgment Seat of Christ takes place only in heaven.

The Criteria for This Judgment

That brings us to the thing we all want to know: What is going to happen at that moment? What will happen when I stand before the Lord on that day? In 1 Corinthians 3:11-15, Paul gives offers a clear illustration of what this judgment will look like. He likens it to a building that is on fire, and after the flames extinguish, the nature of the materials that were used to build the building will be revealed.

One day at the Judgment Seat of Christ, there is going to be a fire, but the fire there will be the white-hot gaze of the eyes of the Lord Jesus Christ. In the Bible, the eyes of Christ are pictured as a blazing fire that penetrates everything (Revelation 1:14). And that fire will sort out all that we have ever done, whether it was for the right reasons or whether it was all for pretend. Fire is a well-known biblical image of testing, and fire will ultimately determine what we have done in our lives as Christians.

The Conclusion of This Judgment

The conclusion of the judgment is twofold. It encompasses both positive and negative events.

1. The Loss of Rewards

The Bible says that some people are going to stand before the Judgment Seat of Christ—where all the rewards are given—and they are not going to receive any reward. They won't have it to lose; they just will lose the opportunity to get one.

Scripture gives us some examples of how and why this happens. In Matthew 6:1, Jesus says, "Take heed that you do not do your charitable deeds before men, to be seen by them. Otherwise you have no reward from your Father in heaven." If you advertise your giving, it is of no credit to you.

Later on in the same passage, Jesus says, "And when you pray, you shall not be like the hypocrites. For they love to pray standing in the synagogues and on the corners of the streets, that they may be seen by men. Assuredly, I say to you, they have their reward" (Matthew 6:5). If you do what you do for the recognition of men and not the glory of God, you will not receive any rewards in heaven. It's that simple.

2. The Reception of Rewards

Throughout God's Word, we are told there are rewards that will be given to us in heaven and that we should endeavor to earn them by our works here on earth. We should be doing all within our ability to extend the Kingdom of God and to make a difference for Christ in our world. You shouldn't be embarrassed to be ambitious to do that, and you shouldn't be embarrassed to be ambitious in storing up for yourself treasures in heaven.

Every day, God gives us opportunities to please Him. Every day God gives us opportunities to make a difference in the Kingdom. And Scripture says that we are stewards of that which

God entrusts to us—and if He has entrusted much to us, much will be required.

But whatever is given to us, God wants us to take it and use it and develop it for the Kingdom. And if we do, one day at the Judgment Seat of Christ, we will be judged, but judged for blessings and rewards. What a good and gracious God we serve!

Notes

1. L. Sale-Harrison, *The Judgment Seat of Christ* (New York, NY: Hephzibah House, 1938), 8.
2. J. Dwight Pentecost, *Prophecy for Today* (Grand Rapids, MI: Zondervan Publishing Company, 1961), 152.

PERSONAL QUESTIONS

1. Read 1 Corinthians 3:8-15.

    a. According to verse 8, each person's award will be given according to what?

    b. As workers of God, Paul likens believers to what two possessions of God? (verse 9)

    c. What work are all believers to take heed of doing? (verse 10)

    d. What is truly the only foundation there is? (verse 11)

    e. What will reveal the true nature of each person's work? (verse 13) How?

    f. What happens if a person's work endures the fire? (verse 14)

The Pretenders • 61

g. What happens if a person's work is burned? (verse 15)

h. Graciously, even if a person's work is lost, what will happen to them personally? (verse 15)

2. Read 2 Corinthians 5:9-11.
    a. According to verse 9, what should be our main goal in life?

    b. List some simple ways you can accomplish this aim in your own life.

    c. Where will all believers make a mandatory appearance? (verse 10)

    d. We will receive judgment for things done where? Why is this such an important distinction? (verse 10)

    e. What kind of deeds will be judged on that day? (verse 10) What is your reaction to that news?

f. With what aspect of God are we able to persuade men? (verse 11) Do we do this today? Explain why or why not.

g. Verse 11 says that we are "well known" to God. How can this fact make an impact on how you live your everyday life? Does it?

3. Read 1 Peter 1:17-19.

   a. Verse 17 says that God judges according to what? And in which way does He do it?

   b. Why do you think God is impartial when it comes to judging us?

   c. List the things that verse 18 states do not redeem us.

   d. In the end, what is the only thing that redeems us? (verse 19)

GROUP QUESTIONS

1. Read Acts 17:30-31 and discuss the following questions.

    a. God once overlooked our ignorance, but now commands us to repent in light of what?

    b. Jesus will judge the world in what? (verse 31) What does that mean?

    c. What did God do to ensure the fact that Jesus will indeed judge the world one day? (verse 31)

    d. Discuss why Jesus' resurrection gives Him the authority to judge all living things. (See John 5:22, 27, and Acts 10:42.)

2. Read 2 Timothy 4:1-5.

    a. As a group list and discuss all the commands that the Christian is to actively follow because of the reality of the coming judgment of Christ.

b. How many of these acts does the modern church execute today? How many does it ignore? Discuss why and what steps can be taken to better live out this passage as a church and as individuals.

c. When people turn away from sound doctrine, what do they turn to? (verses 3-4)

d. How can keeping the coming judgment of Christ always in mind keep us from falling away?

3. Read 1 Peter 4:1-6.

   a. Summarize the main idea of this passage of Scripture.

   b. Discuss why Christ's physical, fleshly suffering is so fundamental to not only our salvation, but also the coming judgment.

The Pretenders • 65

DID YOU KNOW?

The Bible tells us that at the Judgment Seat of Christ, there are five different crowns available as rewards to those who have earned them by their godly endeavors from their earthly life. The five crowns described to us in Scripture are the Victor's Crown, the Crown of Rejoicing, the Crown of Righteousness, the Crown of Glory, and the Crown of Life. But what will we do with our crowns? Revelation 4:10 gives us an idea, for as an act of worship and thanks for all that God has done, we read that the twenty-four elders continually "cast their crowns before the throne."

LESSON 16

Rewards
Heaven's Oscars

Selected Scriptures

In this lesson we learn about the rewards believers will receive in heaven.

OUTLINE

Athletes in ancient Greece practiced for years to win prizes that would soon fade away. Christians who run the spiritual race diligently will receive rewards for their faithfulness at the Judgment Seat of Christ, rewards which they will reinvest in the glory of Christ for eternity.

I. The Day of Heaven's Rewards

II. The Distinction of Heaven's Rewards

III. The Description of Heaven's Rewards
   A. The Victor's Crown
   B. The Crown of Rejoicing
   C. The Crown of Righteousness
   D. The Crown of Life
   E. The Crown of Glory

IV. The Difference Heaven's Rewards Can Make
   A. Remember That the Lord Himself Is Your Chief Reward
   B. Resist Doing Works Outwardly for the Purpose of Receiving a Reward
   C. Reflect Upon the Ultimate Goal of Any Rewards We May Receive

Heaven's Oscars • 67

OVERVIEW

The concept and idea of receiving rewards can be found throughout history. I did a little research and discovered 42 different award shows that are available to be seen each year. There are the Academy Awards, the People's Choice Awards, the Golden Globe Awards, the Screen Actors Guild Awards, the Grammy Awards, the Country Music Association Awards—and the list goes on and on. But there is an award show coming that this world knows nothing of, one that will put all other award shows to shame for its grandeur and the quality of the awards to be given. Those are the rewards given to believers prior to their permanent entrance into heaven.

Some people don't understand the rationale behind Christians getting rewards. They think it sounds like bribing children to be good by offering them candy. Doing and being good, they say, should be their own reward. But the idea of rewards is completely biblical and consistent with God's character as we will see in this lesson.

The concept of rewards is found in the Old Testament (Psalm 58:11; 62:12), and Jesus opens the New Testament era by citing rewards for those persecuted for the sake of righteousness (Matthew 5:11-12). And at the end of the Bible, in Revelation 22:12, we find Jesus saying, "And behold, I am coming quickly, and My reward is with Me...." Rewards are mentioned in many other places in the New Testament: Mark 9:41; 10:29-30; Luke 18:29-30; 1 Corinthians 3:14; Colossians 3:24; Hebrews 6:10-12.

In this lesson, we'll look at the timing and the kinds of rewards God intends to give as part of our entrance into heaven.

THE DAY OF HEAVEN'S REWARDS

Here's the big picture: The Bible says that after all believers, dead and alive, are removed from earth at the Rapture of the Church, believers will be judged individually for their works as Christians; and special rewards will be handed out. Here are excerpts from several Scriptures that address this event:

- Romans 14:12: "So then each of us shall give account of himself to God."
- 2 Corinthians 5:10: "For we must all appear before the judgment seat of Christ."
- Ephesians 6:8: "Knowing that whatever good anyone does, he will receive the same from the Lord."

- 1 Corinthians 3:14: "If anyone's work which he has built on it endures, he will receive a reward."

This judgment has nothing to do with our salvation. Rather it has to do with the kind of Christian we have been, a judgment of our faithfulness as followers of Christ. The penetrating gaze of Christ will look past all our posturing and spin and see us for what we really are. There'll be no excuses or rationalizations. We will stand silently before the Son of God and know that His judgment is wholly true. Whatever rewards we receive (or not) will be totally appropriate. There will be no need for appeals or discussions since His judgments will be perfect.

THE DISTINCTION OF HEAVEN'S REWARDS

The Judgment Seat of Christ is not a final exam to determine your suitability for heaven. Because this judgment does evaluate our works, some have thought it was to determine whether we have enough good works to merit entrance into heaven. That is wrong. The Bible could not be more clear that we are saved by grace, not according to our works (Ephesians 2:8-9; see also Romans 8:1; 1 Corinthians 15:3; 1 John 2:12). If you have trusted Jesus Christ as your Savior, your sins have been forgiven; and that is what qualifies you to enter the holy presence of God in heaven. Your sins—past, present, and future—were paid for on Calvary's cross and will not be a matter of examination at the Judgment Seat of Christ regarding your salvation.

Instead, the Judgment Seat of Christ is where you will be rewarded for your service to the Lord in your Christian experience. This service is a matter of faithfulness on the part of those who are already saved, not works that bear on your salvation. These are the works described in Ephesians 2:10 that follow after our salvation by grace: "For we are His workmanship, created in Christ Jesus for good works, which God prepared beforehand that we should walk in them."

We are not saved by good works, but are saved for good works. This truth has apparently not registered with much of the Christian community since surveys indicate the lifestyles of most Christians are not significantly different from non-Christians. There will be a rude awakening at the Judgment Seat of Christ when many discover there are no rewards given to them.

Bruce Wilkinson has summarized the difference between being saved and being rewarded for service: "Our eternal destination is the consequence of what we believe on earth. Our eternal compensation is the consequence of how we behave on earth."[1]

When you stand before the Judgment Seat of Christ, it's not about getting into heaven. You'll already be there! It's about heaven's evaluation of your faithful service to Christ. The prospect of this coming judgment is what should keep us from judging one another in this life. We are not the judge—Christ is.

THE DESCRIPTION OF HEAVEN'S REWARDS

The New Testament describes five different kinds of rewards, referred to as crowns, that will be given to believers. I do not believe these are all the rewards that will be given, but are representative of the whole range of crowns that will be handed out.

The Victor's Crown

The Victor's Crown is called an "imperishable crown" by Paul and is compared to the perishable wreaths for which athletes competed in the Greek games. There were two athletic festivals in Greece, the Olympic Games and the Isthmian Games, the latter being held at Corinth. Contestants trained vigorously for ten months, and Paul used this training to illustrate the discipline necessary for spiritual success.

Paul's point is that winning requires discipline and training. If athletes worked diligently for months to win a perishable wreath of olive branches, how much more diligently should we work to win an imperishable crown from God?

Training requires the ability to say "No" when necessary—and not just to things that are sinful. As the saying goes, "The good is the enemy of the best." In order to be and do our best for God, it may require choosing to focus only on those things with the highest value in an eternal sense. There are lots of "good" and "better" things in life that can take our focus off the "best," and it is up to us to identify them and choose accordingly. Bible study, evangelism, helping a neighbor in the name of Christ, sacrificing personal desires to free up money for God's work—all of these choices require sacrifice. And when that kind of discipline is exercised, the Victor's Crown is given.

Think of the difference between an athlete and a non-athlete, to continue Paul's illustration. An athlete makes everything subservient to his goal of winning. The non-athlete lets other desires—food, sleep, possessions—take precedence. The spiritual life is no different. Our willingness to submit to the goal of fulfilling Christ's commands will characterize us as a "Victor"—one who strives to win the race. Our goal is to consider our spiritual walk like an athlete considers a race—something to make sacrifices for in order to win.

The Crown of Rejoicing

Paul asked the Thessalonian Christians, "For what is our hope, or joy, or crown of rejoicing?" And his answer is startling: "Is it not even you in the presence of our Lord Jesus Christ at His coming?"

This crown is given to those who are responsible for others standing before Christ at His return—often called the Soul-Winner's Crown. It's the reward given to those who reach out beyond themselves to lead others to heaven.

Christians talk about Jesus to each other often, and that's good. But when is the last time you talked about Jesus to someone who isn't a Christian? Paul's love for the Thessalonians is evident in his two letters for them—they were his hope, his joy, his Crown of Rejoicing.

The Crown of Righteousness

Paul writes these words during the last days of his life: "Finally, there is laid up for me the crown of righteousness, which the Lord, the righteous Judge, will give to me on that Day" (2 Timothy 4:8). He is a prisoner in Rome and knows his days are numbered. But he is content, knowing he has run the race with faithfulness. He looks forward to receiving the Crown of Righteousness that is given "to all who have loved His appearing"—those who have eagerly anticipated the Second Coming of Christ.

Many Christians are so caught up with all the exciting things they're involved in on earth that they have forgotten that earth is not their home. They love their life here and have many places to go, things to do, and people to see before going to heaven. This crown is not for those believers. It is for those who long for heaven, their true home, who long to see the face of their Savior when He comes for them in the clouds.

The Crown of Life

The recipients of this crown are those "who love Him," even, as Revelation says, in the face of death. It is a crown given to those who maintain their love for Christ while enduring and triumphing over persecution and temptation, even martyrdom. Think of the number of Christians we will see wearing this crown in heaven because they gave their life for the sake of Christ throughout the centuries of Church history.

But it's not just martyrs who will receive this crown—it's any who have suffered, endured, persevered, and encouraged others to do so as well, those who have kept the faith when it was costly to do so.

I wonder if the great hymn writer Charles Wesley had this crown in mind when he wrote these words:

"In hope of that immortal crown,
I now the cross sustain.
And gladly wander up and down,
And smile at toil and pain:
I suffer out my three-score years,
Till my Deliverer come,
And wipe away His servant's tears,
And take His exile home."

The Crown of Life—an "immortal crown" given to those who have smiled "at toil and pain" 'til their Deliverer came.

The Crown of Glory

This is a crown I get excited about because it is given to those who are faithful shepherds of the people of God. But it's not just for pastors, elders, deacons, and leaders with visibility in the church. It will be for all those who were shepherds of the sheep at some level—small groups, Sunday school classes, ministry teams, and in other places of ministry. The wounds of sheep continually need to be bound up, and they need to be guided and encouraged along the way. The Crown of Glory is for those who lay down their lives in that calling of leadership.

THE DIFFERENCE HEAVEN'S REWARDS CAN MAKE

Now that we know what the five crowns are that are mentioned in the New Testament, what should we do with this knowledge? What difference should these future rewards make in our present-day relationship with the Lord?

Remember That the Lord Himself Is Your Chief Reward

In Genesis 15:1, we find God making this statement to Abram: "Do not be afraid, Abram. I am your shield, your exceedingly great reward." God was making great promises to Abram in those days about his future, and it would have been possible to be both fearful of the future and prideful about the blessings God was going to bestow. But God reminds Abram that He, God, is Abram's true reward. Land and descendants and blessing would be nothing apart from God in his life.

Resist Doing Works Outwardly for the Purpose of Receiving a Reward

There is enough of the flesh left in us to be tempted, like an immature child, to be obedient for the purpose of gaining a reward. That kind of insincere play-acting drew some strong words from Jesus when He saw it in the religious community of His day: "Take heed that you do not do your charitable deeds before men, to be seen by them. Otherwise you have no reward from your Father in heaven" (Matthew 6:1). He went on to say that our good deeds ought to be done in secret if we want God the Father to reward us for them.

If we are serving the Lord only to get a reward, we have totally misunderstood Christianity. Our motive for serving should be the same as His motive for saving: LOVE! Rewards are simply God's expressions of joy in response to our love for Him. I have never heard anyone say that they are serving God wholeheartedly in order that they can get a great reward when they get to heaven. Because that is a self-serving notion, you couldn't be serving the Lord while thinking that way.

Reflect Upon the Ultimate Goal of Any Rewards We May Receive

Finally, and most important, we need to stay continually aware of what we will ultimately do with the crowns we receive in heaven. We read in Revelation 4:10-11 that the 24 elders, who represent the Church in heaven, "cast their crowns before the throne, saying: 'You are worthy, O Lord, to receive glory and honor and power; for You created all things, and by Your will they exist and were created.'"

After we receive our crowns as rewards in heaven, we're going to be so excited about the privilege of having served Jesus that we're going to fall down at His feet and offer them back to Him as offerings of worship and praise. He gave His best to bring us to heaven, and we'll offer our best back to Him for the privilege of being there.

Don't miss out on that amazing experience. Live wholeheartedly for Christ for the rest of your life so you will have a crown to cast at His feet.

Note

1. Bruce Wilkinson, A *Life God Rewards: Why Everything You Do Today Matters Forever* (Sisters: Multnomah Press, 2002).

PERSONAL QUESTIONS

1. Read Romans 2:1-11.

   a. What is the overriding message of verses 1-3 concerning judgment? (Is there anyone who will escape God's judgment?)

   b. What does the postponement of God's judgment demonstrate about Him? (verse 4)

   c. What is the postponement of judgment supposed to accomplish in us? (verse 4)

   d. What are those who refuse to repent "treasuring up" for themselves? (verse 5)

   e. What is God's principle employed in all judgment? (verse 6; see Galatians 6:7)

f. What will those who do good receive as a reward? (verses 7, 10)

g. What will the disobedient receive as a reward? (verses 8-9)

h. How do we know there is no partiality with God? (verses 10-11)

2. Turn to 1 Corinthians 9:25-27.
   a. Though all have sinned and fall short of God's glory, what will those who seek to fulfill Christ's commands on earth receive in heaven? (verse 25)

b. Which crown will those "who love Him" receive? (James 1:12)

3. What does Matthew 6:1 advise against?

   a. Have you ever been at fault for doing this while performing a good deed?

   b. What is the ultimate reason believers will receive crowns in heaven? (See Revelation 4:10-11.)

GROUP QUESTIONS

1. As a group, how do you reconcile Romans 2:7, 10 with Romans 3:10-18? In other words, has anyone ever performed enough good works to receive a righteous reward?

    a. So how do those who want to do good (but often fail) ever receive a righteous reward? (Romans 3:22-23)

2. The "harvest principle" of Galatians 6:7 governs our activity on earth and God's response to it. What does this principle state?

    a. What is God's eternal response to man? Read Romans 6:20-23. (Those who have been set free receive_____. For the lost, the wages of sin is_____.)

    b. How are those rewards experienced in this life, before eternity? (Galatians 6:8)

3. Turn to the section "The Description of Heaven's Rewards." Discuss the reason each of these crowns will be given in heaven:

   a. The Victor's Crown (1 Corinthians 9:25-27):

   b. The Crown of Rejoicing (1 Thessalonians 2:19):

   c. The Crown of Righteousness (2 Timothy 4:8):

   d. The Crown of Life (James 1:12; Revelation 2:10):

   e. The Crown of Glory (1 Peter 5:4):

4. Read 1 Corinthians 3:11-15 together.

   a. Christians will be judged in spite of having received the gift of salvation freely. What will be the basis of their judgment? (verses 11-13)

   b. If a Christian's work survives the judgment, what will happen? (verse 14)

   c. If their work doesn't survive the judgment, what will happen to them and their work? (verse 15)

DID YOU KNOW?

The Romans used a "judgment seat" (Greek *bema*) for dispensing judgments at trials or for making official pronouncements. Pontius Pilate sat down on a *bema* at the trial of Jesus in Jerusalem (Matthew 27:19), and Paul was brought before the judgment seat of Gallio in Corinth (Acts 18:12). Herod delivered a speech in Caesarea from the *bema* (Acts 12:21), the same one used by Festus when he interrogated Paul years later (Acts 25:6). The idea of the *bema* as a place of judgment for Christians was used twice by Paul, calling it "the judgment seat of Christ" (See Romans 14:10).

LESSON 17

WORSHIP
WORSHIP IN HEAVEN

Revelation 4:1-11

In this lesson we discover the priority of worship in heaven.

OUTLINE

While there is a proliferation of worship music today, some Christians see worship as optional. The apostle John looked through a doorway into heaven and saw that worship was a central activity. The Christian's life should be a dress rehearsal on earth for an eternity of worship in heaven.

I. The Context of Worship in Heaven

II. The Center of Worship in Heaven

III. The Chorus of Worship in Heaven

IV. The Crescendo of Worship in Heaven

V. The Contrast of Worship in Heaven
   A. Worship Is Not About Us—It's About Him
   B. Worship Is Not About Here—It's About There
   C. Worship Is Not About Now—It's About Then
   D. Worship Is Not About One—It's About Many

OVERVIEW

Wheaton College, in Wheaton, Illinois, outside Chicago, was for many years the bastion of Christian higher education in America. There are many fine Christian colleges now, but Wheaton was one of the first and remains one of the best.

For many years, the president of Wheaton College was Ray Edman, a godly man and great leader. In 1967, Dr. Edman was preaching a sermon to the students in the chapel at Wheaton on the subject of worship. He told the students about having met the king of Ethiopia once, and how he had to conform to strict protocols when going into the presence of that earthly king. He told the students that when they came into the presence of the Lord, they needed to come in a manner worthy of the King of kings to worship.

Suddenly, in the middle of his sermon on worship, Dr. Edman collapsed and entered into the presence of the Lord he loved to worship. More than one writer commented after Dr. Edman's death that he would likely have had as seamless a transition from earth to heaven as anyone could imagine. He so loved and worshiped God while on earth that entering into an environment of worship in heaven would be no shock to his system at all.

Today in worship we experience it in three parts: praise of God, prayer to God, and preaching about God. But in heaven only one of those will remain: praise of God. There will be no need to pray since we will be in God's presence with all our needs met. And there won't be preaching in heaven because we will have a complete grasp of the truth about God. Therefore, praise is all that will remain. And the Bible says we will spend eternity in that activity.

Our goal on earth should be like that of Dr. Edman: to prepare ourselves for a seamless transition into the worship environment of heaven by creating that kind of environment on earth. What we learn to do in our short time on earth will prepare us for an eternity in heaven.

In this lesson we will look at Revelation 4:1-11, a central passage on the worship of God in heaven.

THE CONTEXT OF WORSHIP IN HEAVEN

In John's vision, he saw a door standing open, giving him a vision into heaven. Through that door he saw something no one on earth had ever seen before: worship in heaven.

John, along with Peter and James, was part of Jesus' inner circle of disciples. He was with Jesus on the Mount of Transfiguration, in the Garden of Gethsemane, at the Crucifixion, and at the Resurrection. But in addition to these high moments in his life, John had also suffered for Jesus. In fact, when he received the vision of heaven, he was on the island of Patmos in the Mediterranean where he had been exiled by the Roman emperor (Revelation 1:9). John no doubt wondered if he was going to be killed or left on Patmos to die. It was a difficult time in his life and as a disciple of Christ.

But in the midst of that difficult time, he experienced something that no one else ever had. Perhaps the vision of heaven came at a time when he was at a low point, wondering how he would survive. Suddenly a door was opened and he found himself peering through a portal into heaven itself. I simply am at a loss for words to describe what John must have thought and felt at that moment.

THE CENTER OF WORSHIP IN HEAVEN

The key word in these two verses is the word "throne." In fact, it might be the key word in all the book of Revelation since it occurs more than forty times. "Throne" in Revelation speaks of sovereignty, authority, rule, and control. It speaks of the fact that, while on earth things may appear to be out of control, there is One in heaven who is controlling all things for His purposes.

Sometimes it appears that circumstances in our life are out of control, just as they might appear to one who lives on the earth during the Great Tribulation. But they are not. God is on His throne in heaven working out all things by His plan and for His glory.

The Bible says, "No man shall see [God], and live" (Exodus 33:20). Therefore, when John looked into heaven, he only saw the appearance of God and tried to put it into words as best he could: "like a jasper and a sardius stone in appearance; and there was a rainbow around the throne, in appearance like an emerald." A jasper stone is what we know as a diamond, and the sardius is our ruby. So John saw a brilliant, multifaceted stone that sparkled in the light. Somehow, what John saw was best described in terms of brilliance, worth, beauty, and light. Who among us could have described it any better? It is hard to find words in any human language to describe the appearance of God. All John could do, and all we can do, is describe the impact of His presence, not His person. Describing God is like describing the wind—the best we can do is describe the presence or impact or appearance of the wind, not the wind itself.

Worship in Heaven • 83

The Chorus of Worship in Heaven

By looking into heaven and seeing the throne of God, John became an unwitting observer of worship in heaven. It becomes apparent from his description that, where the throne of God is, there is worship.

John sees 24 additional thrones around the central throne of God on which were seated 24 elders, representatives of the Church of the living God. There were also four living creatures around the throne who continually praised God. And when the creatures praised God, the 24 elders fell from their thrones and cast their crowns before the throne of God and worshiped Him. I cannot even imagine what that must have sounded like—multiply the "Hallelujah Chorus" from Handel's *Messiah* by infinity, and maybe it would come close!

William Temple has defined praise like this, which must be what happens in heaven: "To worship is to quicken the conscience by the holiness of God, to feed the mind with the truth of God, to purge the imagination with the beauty of God, to open the heart to the love of God and to devote the will to the purpose of God."[1] This should be the goal of every worshiper on earth as we prepare to worship before the throne of God in heaven.

The Crescendo of Worship in Heaven

"Crescendo" basically means to start small and end big, usually applied to pieces of music. In the worship songs in Revelation there is an obvious crescendo that grows throughout the book. In Revelation 1:6 there is a two-fold doxology; in 4:11 there is a three-fold doxology; in 5:13 there is a four-fold doxology. Then, when you get to 7:12 there is a seven-fold doxology: "Amen! Blessing and glory and wisdom, thanksgiving and honor and power and might, be to our God forever and ever. Amen."

The worship grows as you move through the book—a crescendo of worship to the Lord. When church choirs do that—start soft and simple and end loud and complex—it's biblical!

There's another aspect of crescendo we should consider: It's as if the crescendo of worship for God escalates in accord with the timeline of God's purposes in the world. In other words, the farther along God's timeline of history we go, the greater becomes the praise and worship for Him. There has never been in the history of Christianity an emphasis on praise and worship like there is today. Christian radio stations can't play enough praise and worship music. Churches are incorporating more of it into their services.

And CDs and DVDs of praise and worship are filling the store shelves. If what I'm suggesting is accurate, this crescendo of praise and worship we are experiencing is in accord with His timeline because we are getting ever closer to the "grand finale" of His purposes on earth, ultimately culminating with the praise of God in heaven.

THE CONTRAST OF WORSHIP IN HEAVEN

In C. S. Lewis's allegory *The Great Divorce*, he tells of a man who journeys to heaven and finds it to be grander in scale and more beautiful than he could have imagined. Hell, he discovers, is the opposite, a fleck of dust by comparison with heaven. In the same way, Lewis suggests our lives in this world get smaller and smaller the more we comprehend the grandeur of heaven and eternity.[2] Seeing heaven was for John like us walking up to the edge of the Grand Canyon for the first time—speechless in wonder.

John experienced smallness and largeness at the same time on Patmos. He was probably discouraged and despairing in light of his personal circumstances. But then he was given a view of the grandeur of heaven and the majesty of heavenly worship. And he was changed. When he saw that all of heaven and earth were under the authority of God in heaven, he was able to look at his exile on Patmos in a new light. Seeing our lives against the backdrop of heaven is the best way to keep things in perspective.

By necessity, our lives are focused continually on the present— the things of this world. We face demands in life that require us to focus on the here-and-now. Yet heaven is no less real than this present world. In fact, it is even more real in an ultimate sense. This world is passing away, but heaven will last forever. When John's temporal world and circumstances were ushered into the presence of God, he was reminded that there is something bigger and more important than the day-to-day. He remembered that God is able to do above and beyond what we can ask and think or expect (Ephesians 3:20). He remembered that nothing is impossible for God (Luke 1:37).

We can be reminded of those same truths through worship. We may not see into heaven with our eyes, but we see the character of God through His Word and our songs of praise that proclaim His

Worship in Heaven • 85

worthiness. We can hear Jesus remind us of the same things of which He reminded John: "John, I want you to know that things are not as they appear to be. I'm going to show you how things really are. I'm going to walk you into the throne room of heaven and show you genuine reality. Things are not out of control. Satan has not won. Evil has not triumphed. Peek through the door; get a glimpse of reality. God is on His throne, and such a sight will transform your heart and your mind forever."

Here are four things that we can learn from John's experience on the isle of Patmos.

Worship Is Not About Us— It's About Him

This is easy to forget—God is the center of our worship. It's amazing how many people in churches never get their attention centered on God because they don't like the hymns, the music, the style of worship, the personality of the worship leader, the color of the choir robes or hymn books, and a hundred other things. As a result, they make worship all about them instead of about God.

When you go into a worship service with the conscious intent to praise and worship God for who He is and what He has done, you will have blinders on that keep you from seeing all the stuff you don't like. Worship isn't about those things. It's about God.

Worship Is Not About Here— It's About There

For God, worship exalts and extols His majesty. But for us, worship gets our minds off the things of this earth and onto the realities in heaven. The only way we can live our life on earth with the values and priorities of heaven is to continually focus on heaven. If all we ever see with our spiritual eyes are the carnal and worldly affairs of this life, we will struggle. But if we are continually reminded of God's character, His purposes and plans, and His love for us, then we walk through this world with a different gait. Colossians 3:1–3 reminds us to seek and set our minds on things above. We are citizens of heaven, and that is to be the focus of our eyes and ears and the desire of our heart.

Worship Is Not About Now— It's About Then

Paul writes in 2 Corinthians 4:16-18 that we are to look not "at the things which are seen, but at the things which are not seen. For the things which are seen are temporary, but the things which are not seen are eternal." Paul is encouraging the Corinthians (and us) to leverage everything going on in their lives against the promise of the future. The contrasts he draws in these verses are powerful: The outward man is perishing, but the inward man is being renewed. The affliction of today is light, but the weight of future glory is heavy. The things that are seen are temporal, but the things that are unseen are eternal. Worship is the corridor through which we exchange the things of this world—affliction, suffering, limitations—for the reality of heaven.

Worship Is Not About One— It's About Many

We live in a day when people don't believe they need to worship in church with the Body of Christ. People claim they can worship in nature or on the golf course on Sunday morning. In the book of Revelation, what we see in heaven is corporate worship. Christianity is not an individual experience. Yes, we are saved individually, but immediately we are baptized into the Body of Christ where we remain for eternity. I cannot encourage you enough to make sure that you learn to do on earth what you will be doing for eternity in heaven: worship with the many that God has redeemed for Himself.

Because we don't know the day or hour when we will be promoted to heaven, I encourage you to make every day a full dress rehearsal for the worship that will characterize your eternal life.

Notes

1. Erwin Lutzer, *Pastor to Pastor* (Grand Rapids: Kregel Inc., 1998), 79.
2. C. S. Lewis, *The Great Divorce* (UK: Geoffrey Bles, 1945), n.p.

PERSONAL QUESTIONS

1. Compare the last line of Revelation 4:8 with Exodus 3:14. How is the phrase "was and is and is to come" another way of saying "I am"?

   a. How is this confession in Revelation 4:8 a statement about the sovereignty of God throughout human history? Is there any time in which He is not "Almighty"?

   b. Write out a statement of your own, giving God "glory and honor and thanks." (Revelation 4:9)

   c. What is one reason for giving God "glory and honor and power"? (Revelation 4:11)

   d. What does that say to you about your stewardship of what God has created? (Genesis 1:28)

2. How many thrones did John see around the central throne of God? (Revelation 4:4)

   a. Who were seated on those thrones?

   b. What was their purpose? (Revelation 4:9-11)

3. In heaven there is continual praise while on earth there is not. Are you prepared for that transition? Do you look forward to it? Explain.

   a. In what ways can you prepare for an eternity of worship in heaven, while here on earth, according to Colossians 3:1-3?

   b. In 2 Corinthians 4:16-18, what does Paul encourage believers to do in order for us not to lose heart? (verse 18)

GROUP QUESTIONS

1. Read Revelation 4:8-11 as a group.

   a. Note the similarities in appearance between the four creatures John saw and the seraphim Isaiah saw in their visions of God on His throne. (Isaiah 6:2)

   b. What were the seraphim in Isaiah's vision doing with their six wings? (Isaiah 6:2)

   c. What reasons can you suggest for the seraphs covering their faces and feet? Of what might these acts be symbols?

   d. Why do you think the creatures in John's vision had so many eyes? (Revelation 4:8)

   e. What is the significance of their continual (day and night) praise to God? (verse 8)

f. How do their words provide continuity with the seraphim in Isaiah's vision? (Isaiah 6:3; Revelation 4:8)

g. What significance do you find in the seraphim calling to one another instead of directing their praise to God? (Isaiah 6:3)

h. What practical example do you find in this? What value is there in confessing our beliefs about the character of God to one another?

i. Is the earth "full of His glory" at present, or are these merely prophetic words of the seraphim? (Isaiah 6:3)

j. What value do you see in confessing what you know the future holds, even though it has not yet appeared?

Worship in Heaven • 91

DID YOU KNOW?

The creatures seen by Isaiah are called seraphim by the prophet (Isaiah 6:2; "seraph" is singular, "seraphim" is plural, "im" being the plural ending in Hebrew). Isaiah's vision is the only place in Scripture where heavenly creatures are called seraphim. The Hebrew root "srp," from which seraph likely comes, means to burn. It also is the basis for the word *serpent,* as in the bronze serpent Moses mounted on a pole in Numbers 21:8-9 to save Israel from the bites of the "fiery [srp] serpents" among them (Numbers 21:6). Were the seraphim in Isaiah's vision serpentine-shaped creatures? Images of winged serpents have been uncovered by archaeologists from the Old Testament era, but it is impossible to tell if Isaiah's seraphim had that shape.

LESSON 18

FOUR RIDERS
THE FOUR HORSEMEN OF THE APOCALYPSE

Revelation 6:1-8

In this lesson we learn how a fourth of the world's population will be destroyed in the Tribulation.

OUTLINE

A cursory look around our globe reveals some terrifying realities—war, starvation, diseases with no cure, uncontrollable dictators, biological terrorism. Some might think the Tribulation has already begun. In reality, these are just birth pangs of something much worse to come.

I. The First Seal Opened: The White Horse

II. The Second Seal Opened: The Red Horse

III. The Third Seal Opened: The Black Horse

IV. The Fourth Seal Opened: The Pale Horse

V. Conclusion
   A. The Response of Praise
   B. The Response of Passion
   C. The Response of Personal Evaluation

OVERVIEW

We have arrived in our study at Revelation 6—the place where the real action of the Great Tribulation begins. Chapter 1 contained the things John saw, chapters 2–3 the things which are, and chapters 4–5 the setting of the throne of God in heaven from which the judgments of the Tribulation will proceed. Held in the hand of the One on the throne is a scroll which is taken by the Lamb who was slain (5:7). That scroll contains seven seals, the seventh of which contains seven trumpets, the seventh of which contains seven bowls—judgments all, about to fall upon the earth.

It will take three lessons in our series to cover all of Revelation 6. In this first lesson of the three, we will cover Revelation 6:1-8 and discover the content of the first four seals which are opened by Christ. The first four seals consist of four horsemen who are released to ride upon the earth, carrying various forms of judgment. In our day, the relevance of the horse as a metaphor for judgment is unfamiliar. But in the biblical world, the horse would have been readily understood. For example, Job 39:19-25 is an extended reference to the esteem in which horses were held in the ancient world. In battle, the strength and fearlessness of the horse was respected. The horse was primarily thought of as a weapon of war more than as an agricultural asset or mode of transportation. So the image of four horsemen would bring to mind immediately the idea of warfare and battle to the ancient reader of Revelation.

Four times (6:1, 3, 5, 7) we read the word, "Come!" Most translations have this command directed to John—but he is already there. It seems better to read the word with its alternate meaning, "go" or "proceed," and have it directed to the four horsemen. Therefore, the living creature issuing the command sends each of the four horsemen out of heaven to their mission on earth—"Go!"

THE FIRST SEAL OPENED: THE WHITE HORSE

The white horse (verse 2) in oriental imagery was the picture of a conqueror. Since it is the first horse sent out at the beginning of the Tribulation period, we must discover the purpose and meaning of this first horseman. Because there is a reference to Christ riding a white horse in Revelation 19:11, some believe that Christ Himself must be the rider on this white horse. But there are some differences which make that conclusion strained, at best. Consider the differences:

- Chapter 19, Christ's weapon is a sword; chapter 6, the rider's weapon is a bow with no arrows.
- Chapter 19, Christ wears a crown (a diadem, or kingly crown); chapter 6, the rider wears a stephanzos, a victor's crown of one going forth to conquer. It could be worn by anyone, whereas the diadem can only be worn by Christ.
- Chapter 19, the white horse signals the end of judgment; chapter 6, the white horse signals the beginning of judgment. It isn't likely that Christ would appear in both places, especially since His Second Coming is the more logical place for Him to appear to put an end to judgment.

These and other disparities between the two riders lead me to believe that the rider of the white horse in Revelation 6 is not Christ, but the Antichrist. He carries no arrows because we know he conquers in the name of false peace. He is the prince mentioned in Daniel 9:26 who makes a covenant with Israel to protect the Jews from their enemies. This treaty marks the beginning of the Great Tribulation. The next horseman (verse 4) is allowed to "take peace from the earth," the peace which the first horseman, the Antichrist, has established.

The person represented by the rider on the white horse could be alive in our world today since he will appear at the beginning of the Tribulation as a full-grown man. That means he would have been born thirty to fifty years prior to his appearance at the beginning of the Tribulation. Many believe the world stage is set for the appearance of such a person, meaning he could be alive at this moment.

THE SECOND SEAL OPENED: THE RED HORSE

It is very clear that the rider on the second horse personifies war; its red color (verses 3-4) speaks

> *In the restlessness of nations and in the revolution of the masses and in the prospect of catastrophic war, the first thing that will happen is to be the appearance of this great, final dictator, this great, final world-tyrant. He will promise peace and he will bring with him every token of affluence and prosperity; and the nations of the world and the peoples of the earth will flock after him. This is our Führer, this is our great leader, this is our saviour and the hope of the world. He comes riding on a white horse, conquering and to conquer. The entire military and economic and political resources of the world are at his disposal.*
>
> W. A. Criswell

clearly of the shedding of blood. War is nothing new to the human race; thousands and thousands of conflicts fill the pages of recorded human history. In the last hundred years alone, two world wars claimed the lives of 42 million people with 50 million more being wounded. Millions more civilians were killed or died in concentration camps. But the wars yet to be fought on planet earth, and the suffering which attends war, will be more devastating than anything in history. The "great sword" the rider holds in his hand is the large sword used by Roman soldiers going into battle—used when nations rise against nations.

You may ask why it is important to know about these four horsemen if, as a Christian, I am going to be absent from the earth during the period of the Tribulation. The reason is that every event casts its shadow before it. That which will take place in the future has its portents in the present. The "wars and rumors of wars" (Matthew 24:6) we hear of today are the foretastes of that which is yet to come—and those foretastes are part of the diet of the world each of us lives in today.

As wars and conflicts increase, the world will become restless for someone to bring peace and unity to our divided and embattled world. And it is in that context that the Antichrist will arise. There will be a thin dividing line between the signs of the appearing of the Antichrist and his actual inauguration as a world leader. Between those two events, the Rapture of the Church will occur. But the Church may be on earth during a significant part of the turmoil leading up to the revealing of the Antichrist. That is why it is important to know the stages of judgment represented by the four horsemen.

THE THIRD SEAL OPENED: THE BLACK HORSE

The color black is often connected with death and starvation, and famine often occurs as a result of war. Scarcity of food and other resources often result in an increase in prices so that enough food to subsist on can consume all of one's daily wages. Verse 6 indicates that a quart of wheat, or three quarts of barley (enough for one day), would cost a denarius (penny), which constituted a day's wage in biblical times. In the Tribulation period, along with the appearance of the Antichrist followed by war, famine will appear, and the globe will be wrenched with hunger because of the inability to secure food. All but the rich will suffer, for their staples, oil and wine, will not be harmed. But the average person will border on starvation.

This setting also plays directly into the hands of the Antichrist. Revelation 13:17 says that "no one may buy or sell except one who has the mark or the name of the Beast, or the number of his name." The Beast will control the world through the world's own hunger. Men and nations will do unusual and unplanned things in order to get food—and unfortunately, individuals will as well. Hunger is a basic human motivation, and the Antichrist will use it to his advantage as a means of moving people to give him allegiance.

> *By forcing on mankind more and more legal weapons and at the same time making the world more and more independent economically, technology has brought mankind to such a degree of distress that we are ripe for the deifying of any new Caesar who might succeed in giving the world unity and peace.*
>
> Arnold Toynbee

We see evidences of the politicization of food distribution in some African countries today. The pathetic and heart-wrenching photos we see of starving children and adults (many of them Christians) make us think in terms of food shortages. In reality, what has sometimes happened is that food supplies have been cut off by warring political factions. As the African proverb has stated for generations, "When elephants battle, the ants get trampled." Using starvation as a means of genocide is a twenty-first century reality in our world. If it is happening today, how much more might it continue at the hand of an evil world ruler?

THE FOURTH SEAL OPENED: THE PALE HORSE

The three previous horses each had one rider only. Now John looks and sees that the fourth horse has a rider with another person following (verses 7-8). Death is the rider with Hades following close behind. Death and Hades are mentioned three times in Revelation. Christ has the keys to Death and Hades in 1:18, and 20:14 says that Death and Hades will be cast into hell. But 20:13 tells us a little more about them. They will be judged one day, following the Tribulation during which they have reigned. They will be judged, "each one according to his works." Found guilty, they will be cast into hell.

After the Antichrist's brief treaty of peace comes war, and after war comes famine, and after famine comes Death and Hades. They are armed with the sword, hunger, pestilence (plagues), and wild beasts. These are the four judgments the Lord said he would send in Ezekiel 14:21. In our day, we have seen war and famine wreak havoc on our world, and we are now in the process of seeing pestilence and beasts and plague do the same. Pestilence is a word for "epidemic." One epidemic that affected millions of people globally is the HIV/AIDS virus. Since its inception, more than 35 million people have died from AIDS. The incubation period of the HIV virus can be from six months up to ten years, so many people who were infected (HIV-positive) did not know it—and unknowingly transmitted the disease—if they had not been tested. As a result, the disease continued to spread until treatments and widespread testing become available. Today we are encountering the global plaque of COVID that has shaken our world with a virus that was unknown to us a few years ago, robbing families of loved ones in every country across the globe. These pandemics or "pestilence" are similar to what we read about in Revelation.

Diseases are also spread by "beasts" of the earth—which could be anything from rats, which can carry as many as 35 known diseases, to disease-resistant microorganisms spread by birds and animals which are shipped or which migrate from one country to another. In past decades and centuries, diseases could be contained in their country of origin fairly easily. But today, a person can contract an animal-borne disease in one country and arrive by airplane in another country in a matter of hours—and be "lost" among the population.

It is not difficult to imagine that "Death" and "Hades" will account for 25 percent of the world's population being killed during the Tribulation (6:8).

CONCLUSION

The Response of Praise

Neither is it difficult to see why praise and worship are the central focus of chapters 4 and 5 of Revelation. Why? Because those who know the Lord Jesus Christ as Savior and Lord will be worshiping Him in heaven while the events of Revelation 6–19 are unfolding on the earth. If being excluded from the fourth of the world's population killed by war, hunger, disease, and the beasts of the earth isn't a reason to praise, I don't know what is.

The Response of Passion

But there is another response we should have. It would be selfish and self-centered for us to be concerned only about saving ourselves. If there is any "neighbor" whom we are to love as we love ourselves, we must warn them of what is coming upon the earth. If we really believe the messages of the four horsemen, we will tell anyone and everyone how they can be spared from the torment of the Tribulation.

The Response of Personal Evaluation

Which brings us to the necessary question, where will you be when Revelation 6 begins to unfold on the earth? Don't wait another minute before making sure that when the trumpet of the Lord sounds, you will leave this earth at the Rapture. After that trumpet, after the Church is gone, it will be too late to reconsider.

PERSONAL QUESTIONS

1. Read Matthew 24:3-15.

    a. What question do the disciples have for Jesus? (verse 3)

    b. How does verse 5 parallel the notion of an Antichrist coming into the world?

    c. Which of the four horsemen in Revelation 6:1-8 could fulfill the sign Jesus mentions in verses 6-7?

    d. What is the parallel between verse 7 and the horseman in Revelation 6:5-6?

    e. What does verse 9 suggest about when these events will begin—that is, the relation of these events to the Rapture of believers?

f. What is characteristic of birth pangs? That is, do they begin slowly and gradually increase or arrive suddenly with full intensity? What does this suggest as to the timing of these events in relationship to the Rapture?

2. Read Matthew 24:32-35.

   a. What sign is evident on a fig tree with regard to the approach of summer? (verse 32)

   b. What should the disciples of Jesus learn from this parable with regard to the end of the age? (verse 33)

   c. What generation did Jesus refer to in verse 34—the generation to which He was speaking or the generation that sees the beginning of the signs He has described?

   d. How certain can we be that the signs (including the four horsemen of Revelation 6) will come to pass? (verse 35)

The Four Horsemen of the Apocalypse • 101

GROUP QUESTIONS

1. Read Revelation 6:1-8 and discuss the following questions: What do each of the horses and riders personify? What event does each bring to the world? Explain your reasoning for each answer.

   a. The rider on the white horse (verse 2)

   b. The rider on the red horse (verse 4)

   c. The rider on the black horse (verses 5-6)

   d. The rider on the pale horse (verse 8)

   e. What did horses signify in the ancient world? Using that definition, what would the image of four horsemen bring to mind?

2. What evidence do you see in our world today that might be signs of the presence of these four horsemen?

   a. The rider on the white horse (verse 2)

   b. The rider on the red horse (verse 4)

   c. The rider on the black horse (verses 5-6)

   d. The rider on the pale horse (verse 8)

3. Why is it important to study the four horsemen when, as Christians, we will not be present for the Great Tribulation?

   a. What is our calling as we await the Great Tribulation?

The Four Horsemen of the Apocalypse • 103

DID YOU KNOW?

The four horsemen of the Apocalypse, described in Revelation 6:1-8, have become cultural icons and models through the centuries. Their title has been applied to characters in computer games, rock bands, rock songs, NASA scientists during the Apollo era, Supreme Court justices during the New Deal era of Franklin Roosevelt, a group of atheist scientists, professional wrestlers, and a group of computer scientists. The most well-known group were the four members of the backfield on the Notre Dame University football team, coached by the legendary Knute Rockne, in 1924. All are examples of how the truth of Scripture can be diluted by cultural misuse.

LESSON 19

ANTICHRIST
THE BEAST FROM THE SEA

Selected Scriptures

In this lesson we learn about the character and future activities of the coming Antichrist.

OUTLINE

History is full of the accounts of presumptuous leaders who perpetrated "crimes against humanity" for the sake of their own agendas. But no prior leader will compare, in arrogance or evil, with the soon to come Antichrist who will eventually rule the world with an iron fist.

I. His Preparation

II. His Presentation

III. His Personality

IV. His Plan

V. His Pride

VI. His Peace Treaty

VII. His Persecutions

VIII. His Power

IX. His Profaneness

X. His Punishment

OVERVIEW

It is reported that the former prime minister of Belgium, P. H. Spaak, made the following statement:

> The truth is that the method of international committees has failed. What we need is a person, someone of the highest order, of great experience, of great authority, of wide influence, of great energy. Let him come and let him come quickly. Either a civilian or a military man, no matter what his nationality, who will cut all the red tape, shove out of the way all the committees, wake up all the people and galvanize all governments into action. Let him come quickly. This man we need and for whom we wait will take charge of the defense of the West. Once more I say, it is not too late, but it is high time.[1]

Sentiments like that will make the rise of the Antichrist a welcome event to many when it happens.

While the Antichrist is described in more than one hundred passages of Scripture, the word Antichrist itself occurs in only four verses, each time in the writings of the apostle John. Most of those mentions involve people in John's day who were anti-Christ—they were opposed to Christ and His Gospel (see 1 John 2:18, 22; 4:3; 2 John 7). Only once did John apply the term to *the* Antichrist, the person described in Revelation 13:1-10: "Little children, it is the last hour; and as you have heard that the Antichrist is coming, even now many antichrists have come, by which we know that it is the last hour" (1 John 2:18). There is an anti-Christ spirit at work in the world today that will be manifested fully in *the* Antichrist who will come at the end of the age.

While we cannot know the identity of the Antichrist before he appears, we can know much about him based on more than 25 titles given to him and the hundred-plus times he is mentioned. Underlying everything is this: He is a man empowered and controlled by Satan.

HIS PREPARATION

Daniel 8:23-24 describes him as "a king" having "fierce features," employing "sinister schemes," having power that is not his own, and who prospers, thrives, and destroys. He will come at "the time of the end . . . in the latter time of indignation" (see Daniel 8:17, 19). That last phrase—"the latter time of indignation"—refers to the seven-year period called the Tribulation.

The Antichrist will rise out of the mass of humanity: "And I saw a beast rising up out of the sea" (Revelation 13:1). "Sea" doesn't refer to the ocean but to humanity—specifically, the Gentile nations of the world. This is confirmed in Revelation 17:15 with the phrase: "peoples, multitudes, nations, and tongues."

There are at least four reasons the Antichrist will not be a Jew:

1. Daniel indicates that the Antichrist ("prince") will be from the people that would destroy Jerusalem and the temple (Daniel 9:26). Those people were the Romans under Titus in A.D. 70. Therefore, the Antichrist will be a "Roman," or Gentile.

2. Daniel also saw the Antichrist as the little horn that arose out of 10 horns on the head of the fourth beast that represented the Roman Empire (Daniel 7:7-8, 19-26).

3. John describes the Antichrist as "the beast rising up out of the sea" (Revelation 13:3). In prophecy, the "sea" represents the vast multitudes of Gentile people.

4. He is described as history's most vicious and wicked persecutor of the Jewish people. Gentiles, not Jews, persecute Jews.

HIS PRESENTATION

Second Thessalonians 2:3-4, 7 describes a "falling away" that will take place before the appearing of "the man of sin" (the Antichrist). The word for "falling away" is the word from which we get "apostasy." Before the Antichrist will be revealed and the Tribulation begins, there will be a falling away from the faith by true believers. The falling away is more than just a few people; it is a major departure from the faith by a large segment of believing Christianity.

Jesus Himself predicted such a time: "And then many will be offended, will betray one another, and will hate one another. Then many false prophets will rise up and deceive many. And because lawlessness will abound, the love of many will grow cold" (Matthew 24:10-12). And Paul wrote to Timothy about the same occurrence: "in latter times some will depart from the faith." They will "not endure sound doctrine"; they will "turn their ears away from the truth, and be turned aside to fables" (1 Timothy 4:1; 2 Timothy 4:3-4). The present age will not end in a great revival but a great falling away and apostasy.

Nor can the Antichrist appear before "the restrainer is taken out of the way" (2 Thessalonians 2:7). The restrainer is the Holy Spirit who, by virtue of the Rapture of true believers, will be removed from earth. The Holy Spirit presently restrains sin in the world and the Antichrist, the embodiment of sin. But when the Spirit is removed, all hell—literally speaking—will break loose on earth.

His Personality

According to Daniel, the Antichrist will have a "mouth speaking pompous words . . . against the Most High" (Daniel 7:8, 25). He will "exalt and magnify himself above every god, [and] shall speak blasphemies against the God of gods" (Daniel 11:36). He will be a powerful and charismatic speaker, boasting of his stature above God.

A. W. Pink describes the Antichrist in these terms:

"He will have a mouth speaking very great things. He will have a perfect command and flow of language. His oratory will not only gain attention but respect. Revelation 13:2 declares that his mouth is 'as the mouth of a lion' which is a symbolic expression telling of the majesty and awe-producing effects of his voice."[2]

He will be attractive (Daniel 7:20) and of great intellect (Daniel 8:23, 25). He will possess a stature and magnetism that will draw the world's population to him as leader when things turn bad during the Tribulation period. People will look to him as their only hope.

His Plan

In short, the Antichrist will "seize the kingdom by intrigue" (Daniel 8:25; 11:21). In his dream recorded in Daniel 7, Daniel saw "a little horn, coming up among them before whom three of the first horns were plucked out by the roots" (Daniel 7:8). "Plucked out" refers to push out or cleverly replace. The Antichrist is the little horn who arises among ten others and who subdues three of the ten. The ten are kings—a confederation in the Last Days—among whom the Antichrist will gain prominence (Daniel 7:24). By political intrigue and manipulation, he will eliminate three kingdoms, gathering their power to himself. This is not a sudden coup but a gradual shifting of power. He arises as a minor player among major players and eliminates three of the existing kingdoms in his march to power.

His Pride

"Then he opened his mouth in blasphemy against God, to blaspheme His name, His tabernacle, and those who dwell in heaven" (Revelation 13:6; see also Daniel 11:36-39).

Dr. Henry Morris describes what will motivate the Antichrist's actions:

Not content to rail against God, the dragon-inspired beast must utter diatribes and obscenities against all [God] stands for (His name), defaming His holiness, His love, His law, His grace. He curses the heavens (the dragon has recently been expelled from heaven) where God dwells. Those who dwell with God in heaven, including not only the holy angels but also all the raptured saints, share in his vilifications. This continual barrage of slander must now take place on earth, since the Devil no longer has access to heaven where he used to accuse the brethren."[3]

The Antichrist will acknowledge no religion at all other than the worship of himself and Satan. In his attempt to wipe the thought of God from the world's collective mind, he will try to change the moral and natural laws of the universe: "And shall intend to change time and law" (Daniel 7:25). He will do whatever he can to remove the notion of God from the world.

His Peace Treaty

Daniel 9:27 says the Antichrist will "confirm a covenant with many for one week." This will be a covenant—a peace treaty—with Israel, guaranteeing her protection at the beginning of the Tribulation. Israel will trust in this treaty as a defense from attack by her hostile neighbor nations. He will be seen as the one to finally resolve the Middle East peace problem with this covenant. He will probably be hailed around the world as an international hero, a diplomat of peace.

However, in the middle of the seven-year Tribulation period, the Antichrist will break his covenant and turn against Israel: "But in the middle of the week [after three and one-half years], He shall bring an end to sacrifice and offering. And on the wing of abominations shall be one who makes desolate, even until the consummation, which is determined, is poured out on the desolate" (Daniel 9:27). The Antichrist will turn from being Israel's protector to her persecutor.

His Persecutions

After breaking the treaty he brokered with Israel, the Antichrist will install himself and his image in the Jewish temple. This act of sacrilege marks the beginning of the second half of the Tribulation, often referred to as "The Great Tribulation" (Matthew 24:21). He unleashes his fury upon any who have become Christians during the first half of the Tribulation (remember: the Church was removed from earth before the start of the seven-year period) (Daniel 7:21, 24-25; Revelation 13:7, 16-17).

The word "persecute" literally means "to wear out." The Antichrist's constant persecution and pressure on those who profess faith in God will serve to wear them down. They will be unable to buy food or other necessities because of having refused the mark of the Antichrist. No doubt many will starve to death. Jesus said this period of time will be like nothing in world history (Matthew 24:21-22). John tells us that the Antichrist will be "given authority to continue for forty-two months"—that is, for three-and-one-half years, the second half of the Tribulation period (Revelation 13:5).

Antiochus Epiphanes, a Greek king who ruled the Seleucid Empire in the Middle East from 175-164 B.C., prefigured the behavior of the Antichrist in the way he treated Jews of that period. On one occasion he discovered a number of Jews hiding in a cave, so he lit fires in the cave and sealed the entrance and suffocated all those within. He was a cruel and barbaric ruler, just as the Antichrist will be.

His Power

Paul wrote that the "coming of the lawless one [the Antichrist] is according to the working of Satan, with all power, signs, and lying wonders" (2 Thessalonians 2:9). "Signs and wonders" describes the miraculous works of God throughout Scripture—to include the works of God through Moses (Exodus 7:3), Jesus (Acts 2:22), and the apostles (Acts 2:43). But they are also present in the activity of false prophets (Mark 13:22); thus, the phrase "lying wonders" used by Paul. The purpose of the Antichrist's signs and wonders is to delude people into believing in him. And many will (2 Thessalonians 2:10-12).

When the Antichrist breaks his treaty with Israel, almost simultaneously he will kill God's two true witnesses (Revelation 11:7-8). Also, it will appear as if the Antichrist is killed, but he will come back to life, astonishing the whole world. This will be a gross imitation and counterfeit of the resurrection of Jesus Christ, again in an attempt to establish his credibility (Revelation 13:13). Just as Christ's resurrection caused many to believe, many will give their allegiance to the Antichrist when they see him appear to come back to life.

Remember Paul's description of the Antichrist's work—"according to the work of Satan." The day is coming when God will bring the dead back to life (John 5:28-29) by His divine power. But the Antichrist's return to life will be "according to the work of Satan."

His Profaneness

The result of all the Antichrist's tricks and persecution is that the people worship him: "and they worshiped the beast, saying, 'Who is like the beast? Who is able to make war with him?'" (Revelation 13:4).

The Jews will have rebuilt the temple in Jerusalem by this time, and the Antichrist will have allowed the Jewish worship system to be restarted. But then when he breaks the covenant with Israel, he will surround Jerusalem with his armies and seize control of the city and the temple. And as a final act of presumption the Antichrist will establish himself as God in the temple: "All who dwell on the earth will worship him, whose names have not been written in the Book of Life of the Lamb slain from the foundation of the world" (Revelation 13:8).

The False Prophet will erect a giant image, or statue, of the Antichrist and command everyone to worship it. He will even cause the image to speak! (Revelation 13:14-15) These events are the "abomination of desolation" spoken of by Daniel the prophet (Daniel 11:31; 12:11; Mark 13:14; see also Matthew 24:15).

His Punishment

It is reasonable to ask, What kind of punishment does a man such as the Antichrist deserve? His punishment will come after defying the return of Jesus Christ Himself to earth: "He shall even rise against the Prince of princes, but he shall be broken without human means" (Daniel 8:25).

The Antichrist will gather all the kings of the earth and their armies together to make war against Israel—and then against the returning Christ and His armies from heaven when He appears in the sky (Revelation 19:19; see also Zechariah 12:1-22; 14:1-3; Revelation 16:16). But Christ will be victorious over them all and "consume [them] with the breath of His mouth and . . . the brightness of His coming" (2 Thessalonians 2:8).

The Antichrist will not be annihilated, but he, along with the False Prophet, will be judged and consigned for all eternity to the lake of fire (Revelation 19:20). A thousand years later, at the end of the Millennium, the Antichrist and False Prophet are still alive at which time they will be joined by their mastermind, Satan. "And they will be tormented day and night forever and ever" (Revelation 20:10).

We are surely living in a time when signs are pointing to the events described in this lesson. When world leaders begin to publicly voice a desire for one leader to become a savior for a broken and conflicted world, we know the end is drawing nigh. Every Christian must live daily in preparation for these events, anchoring themselves in a faith that cannot be shaken.

Notes

1. Quoted by Robert Glenn Gromacki, *Are These The Last Days?* (Old Tappan, NJ: Fleming H. Revell Company, 1970), 110.
2. A. W. Pink, *The Antichrist* (Grand Rapids, MI: Kregel Publications reprinted in 1988 from original in 1923), 9.
3. Henry M. Morris, *The Revelation Record* (Wheaton, IL: Tyndale House, Publishers, Inc., 1983), 241.

PERSONAL QUESTIONS

1. Make a note of how the Antichrist is described in each of the following verses and what you think the description conveys about his character or activity:

   a. Daniel 7:8

   b. Daniel 8:23

   c. Daniel 9:26

   d. Daniel 9:27

   e. Daniel 11:36

   f. 2 Thessalonians 2:3

   g. 2 Thessalonians 2:9

h. Revelation 6:2

i. Revelation 13:1

2. Who are the "antichrists" John refers to in 1 John 2:18?

   a. Define the standard John used in 1 John 2:22 to refer to anyone as an antichrist.

   b. What guideline is given in 1 John 4:3?

   c. Based on John's words in 1 John 2:18 and 4:3, what can you assume about the presence of antichrists in the world today?

   d. How should the subject of antichrists impact Christians today? Where should we look for them? How should we measure their words and works? (1 John 4:1)

GROUP QUESTIONS

1. Discuss what two things must happen before the Antichrist is revealed according to 2 Thessalonians 2:3-8:

   a. Event 1: (verse 3)

   b. Event 2: (verse 7)

   c. Why should we not expect a massive revival in the Church of Jesus Christ near the End Times? (See also Matthew 24:10-12; 1 Timothy 4:1; 2 Timothy 4:3-4.)

   d. Who is the "restrainer" that now keeps sin and the Antichrist in check?

   e. If your faith ever begins to grow cold, how should these teachings serve as a warning to you?

2. Why is outward appearance not always a good indication of character? (1 Samuel 9:1-2)

a. What kind of person can easily be drawn to a charismatic, beautiful leader?

b. Compare the appearance and demeanor of Christ (Isaiah 53:2) with that of the Antichrist (Daniel 7:20; 8:23, 25).

c. Discuss why many will give their allegiance to the Antichrist halfway through the Tribulation.

DID YOU KNOW?

The prophet Daniel spoke of the coming Antichrist changing "times and law" as the ruler of the world (Daniel 7:25). Such a radical transformation of societies and commerce would be an attempt to break any and all connections with religious, commercial, and legal precedents, all to be replaced by the Antichrist's rule. This was tried during the French Revolution when, from 1793 to 1805, the French Republican (or Revolutionary) Calendar was instituted. There were still twelve months, but weeks were changed from seven days to ten days. These and many other societal and economic changes were a revolutionary attempt to cut all ties to the previous government and way of life.

LESSON 20

FALSE PROPHET
THE BEAST FROM THE EARTH

Revelation 13:11-18

In this lesson we learn about the satanically inspired man known as the False Prophet.

OUTLINE

No one should doubt the power of religion in human life. Throughout history it has been used to inspire and unite populations. And so it will be during the Tribulation when the Antichrist's spiritual assistant will use his satanic power to promote the worship of the world leader.

I. His Profile

II. His Purpose

III. His Power
    A. Calling Down Fire From Heaven
    B. Commanding That an Image Be Built
    C. Causing the Image to Breathe and Speak

IV. His Program

V. His Punishment

OVERVIEW

It is impossible for us today to know exactly how the False Prophet will rise to power as the spiritual leader and assistant to the Antichrist. But this we know: The book of Revelation makes it abundantly clear that the world will come under the influence, actually the domination, of this satanic duo. The Antichrist will be the supreme ruler of the world, focusing on political and economic unity. The False Prophet will promote spirituality based on the acknowledgement of the "deity" of the Antichrist. The fact that Revelation describes them both as beasts—the Antichrist as a beast from the sea, the False Prophet as a beast from the earth—is all we need to know to imagine their destructive powers.

Today in history no one knows the identity of the two figures, whether they are alive today or not. But the more we know of their future activities, the more readily we will detect the signs of their appearing. In this lesson, we will study the profile, purpose, power, program, and punishment of the False Prophet.

His Profile

John introduces the False Prophet this way: "Then I saw another beast coming up out of the earth, and he had two horns like a lamb and spoke like a dragon" (Revelation 13:11). This person, referred to as a "beast" here, is referred to as the "false prophet" three times in Revelation (16:13; 19:20; 20:10).

John saw two different dimensions of the beast's character: He was both a lamb and a dragon (Revelation 13:11). As a lamb, he was the counterfeit of the Lamb of God who takes away the sins of the world (John 1:29). Jesus warned His disciples about "false prophets, who come to you in sheep's clothing, but inwardly they are ravenous wolves" (Matthew 7:15; see also Matthew 24:11, 24; Mark 13:22; 1 John 4:1).

As a dragon, the False Prophet will be powerful as described by John Phillips:

"The dynamic appeal of the false prophet will lie in his skill in combining political expediency with religious passion, self-interest with benevolent philanthropy, lofty sentiment with blatant sophistry, moral platitude with unbridled self-indulgence. His arguments will be subtle, convincing, and appealing. His oratory will be hypnotic, for he will be able to move the masses to tears or whip them into a frenzy.... His deadly appeal will lie in the fact that what he says will sound so right, so sensible, so exactly what unregenerate men have always wanted to hear."[1]

The term "beast" is applied to Satan, the Antichrist, and the False Prophet in Revelation—a label that binds them together in their destructive aims. These three represent an unholy Trinity—a counterfeit to God the Father, Son, and Holy Spirit. Donald Grey Barnhouse has said: "The devil is making his last and greatest effort, a furious effort, to gain power and establish his kingdom upon the earth. He knows nothing better than to imitate God. Since God has succeeded by means of an incarnation and then by means of the work of the Holy Spirit, the devil will work by means of an incarnation in Antichrist and by the unholy spirit."[2]

HIS PURPOSE

Just as the Holy Spirit's purpose is to exalt the Lord Jesus Christ, so the False Prophet's purpose is to exalt the Antichrist: "And he exercises all the authority of the first beast in his presence, and causes the earth and those who dwell in it to worship the first beast, whose deadly wound was healed" (Revelation 13:12). "As Christ received authority from the Father (Matthew 11:27), so Antichrist receives authority from the dragon (Revelation 13:4), and as the Holy Spirit glorifies Christ (John 16:14), so the false prophet glorifies the Antichrist (Revelation 13:12)."[3]

The False Prophet's goal is to unite the world in a religious spirit to support the Antichrist. Religious leaders have played a major role in the rise and fall of powers throughout world history. W. A. Criswell has written:

"I do not suppose that in the history of mankind, it has ever been possible to rule without religious approbation and devotion.... In the days of Pharaoh, when Moses and Aaron stood before the sovereign of Egypt, he called in Jannis and Jambres, the magicians, the religionists of his day, to oppose Jehovah. When Balak, the king of Moab, sought to destroy Israel, he hired the services of Baalim to curse Israel. When Absalom entered his revolutionary scheme to destroy his own father, David, he did so by the wisdom and advice of Ahithophel.... Ahab and Jezebel were able to do what they did in Israel, in the debauchery of the kingdom, because they were abetted and assisted by the prophets of Baal."[4]

Satan does not love Christianity but he loves religion and will use it to inspire the world to worship the Antichrist under the leadership of the False Prophet.

The Beast From the Earth • 119

HIS POWER

Satan will empower the Antichrist, and the Antichrist will empower the False Prophet to do the following: "He performs great signs . . . in the sight of men. And he deceives those who dwell on the earth by those signs which he was granted to do in the sight of the beast" (Revelation 13:13-14).

Five times in Revelation 13:2-8 we are told the devil gives power to the Antichrist; and three times in Revelation 13:12-15 we learn that the Antichrist gives power to the False Prophet. All the power of the two future leaders originates with Satan. Jesus foretold a day when false prophets would arise and demonstrate great power (Matthew 24:24-25). And the False Prophet is the one in whom Jesus' predictions culminate and are fully expressed.

Just as Satan's goal has been to counterfeit the words and works of the true God (Genesis 3:4-5; 2 Corinthians 11:13-15), so will his chief emissaries on earth seek to counterfeit God on the world stage. The False Prophet will display his counterfeit power in three ways.

Calling Down Fire From Heaven

"He performs great signs, so that he even makes fire come down from heaven on the earth in the sight of men" (Revelation 13:13). This counterfeits the work of God who often displayed His own power with fire from heaven: Fire rained down on Sodom and Gomorrah (Genesis 19:24), fire consumed Nadab and Abihu (Leviticus 10:1-2), and fire will one day destroy Satan's army on earth (Revelation 20:9).

It is also possible that the False Prophet will try to falsely fulfill the prophecy of Malachi 4:5 concerning the coming of Elijah before the day of the Lord. And it was Elijah who called down fire from heaven to consume the prophets of Baal on Mount Carmel (1 Kings 18:38). The False Prophet will try to convince people he is the fulfillment of the Elijah prophecy spoken through Malachi. Scholar Craig S. Keener reminds us that in Scripture prophets are known "by their message and their fruit, not by their gifts [of power] (Deut. 13:1-5; Matt. 7:15-23)."[5]

Commanding That an Image Be Built

The second display of the False Prophet will come by his building "an image to the beast who was wounded by the sword and lived" (Revelation 13:14). This will be a giant statue in honor of the Antichrist —the focal point of false worship on the earth during the seven-year Tribulation (Revelation 13:14, 15; 14:9, 11; 15:2; 16:2; 19:20; 20:4).

This image is likely the object of Jesus' words concerning an "abomination of desolation" in the last days (Matthew 24:15-16, 21). Paul wrote about "the man of sin" exalting himself above God "so that he sits as God in the temple of God, showing himself that he is God" (2 Thessalonians 2:3-4). The image is the public manifestation of the self-exaltation of the Antichrist under the leadership of the False Prophet. The world will be commanded to worship the image much as Nebuchadnezzar commanded in Babylon (Daniel 3).

Causing the Image to Breathe and Speak

One of the most earth-shaking events that will happen is when the False Prophet animates the image set up in honor of the Antichrist. He will "give breath to the image . . . that the image of the beast should . . . speak" (Revelation 13:15). I do not believe this will be done through ventriloquism or animatronics as used at modern theme parks to make "animals" speak. I believe Dr. Henry Morris's explanation is more likely correct:

"The false prophet is enabled (by his own master, Satan) to impart a spirit to the image, but that spirit is one of Satan's unclean spirits, probably a highly placed demon in the satanic hierarchy. This is a striking case of demon possession, with the demon possessing the body of the image rather than that of a man or woman."[6]

Through Satan, the False Prophet will cause an inanimate object to appear to come to life. This is a radical example of the dark spiritual power that will be active during the Tribulation. The image will command the entire world to worship it—that is, to worship the Antichrist—upon pain of death for refusal.

HIS PROGRAM

The False Prophet will tell the world that a mark of obedience to the Antichrist will be necessary to buy or sell in the marketplace: "He causes all, both great and small, rich and poor, free and slave to receive a mark on their right hand or on their foreheads, and that no one may buy or sell except one who has the mark or the name of the beast, or the number of his name" (Revelation 13:16-17).

Revelation 7:3, God's 144,000 Jewish witnesses are sealed on their foreheads as belonging to God, so the Antichrist demands that everyone else in the world display a seal of allegiance to him—on their forehead or their right hand. The mark of the Antichrist will be needed to buy the necessities of life. Often in the Roman Empire a seal of the emperor would be used to stamp official documents and grant the right to conduct commerce.

The cooperation between government and religion will leave no place of refuge for any who rebel. Frederick Tatford says:

"What is portrayed is a tremendous union in which capital and labor are both subject to the control and direction of one man. Anyone who is outside that vast combination will be ruthlessly boycotted; no one will work for him or employ him; no one will purchase his produce or sell goods to him. Bankruptcy and starvation face such a man."[7]

Many are alive in America today who remember the rationing that was in place during World War II. Ration tickets were necessary to buy basic commodities because the war effort greatly reduced the availability of goods. It will be similar in the Tribulation; but instead of being able to buy only a little, people will be able to buy nothing without the mark of the Antichrist showing on forehead or hand.

There is a clue to what the mark will be in Revelation 13:18: "Here is wisdom. Let him who has understanding calculate the number of the beast, for it is the number of a man: His number is 666." In spite of many fanciful suggestions through the ages, no one knows what "666" stands for in terms of the mark of the Antichrist.

The number 6 is associated with man throughout Scripture, and the number 7 is associated with God. In Revelation the number 7 occurs more than 50 times. Six is the number of man, as Revelation 13:18 says, while 7 is the number of God. Six is the number of incompleteness, while 7 is the number of completeness. Perhaps 666 is a symbol of the incompleteness of man's efforts to bring about righteousness and perfection on earth, which is what the Antichrist will try to do. Man always falls short of the glory of God (Romans 3:23).

Donald Grey Barnhouse illustrated why the mark of the Antichrist should create a desire for God, not for man, in us:

"The children of the great composer, Bach, found that the easiest method of awakening their father was to play a few lines of music and leave off the last note. The musician would arise immediately and go to the piano to strike the final chord.

"I awoke early one morning in our home and played the well-known carol 'Silent Night.' I purposely stopped before playing the last note. I walked out into the hallway and listened to the sounds that came from upstairs. My eight-year-old son had stopped reading and was trying to sound the final note on his harmonica. Another child was singing the last note. An adult called down, 'Did you do that purposely? What is the matter?' Our very nature demands the completion of the octave."[8]

As a human man, the Antichrist will never satisfy the world's need for the perfection and completion only God can provide.

His Punishment

We have to skip ahead to the end of Revelation to discover the fate of the False Prophet: "The beast was captured, and with him the false prophet who worked signs in his presence, by which he deceived those who received the mark of the beast and those who worshiped his image. These two were cast alive into the lake of fire burning with brimstone" (Revelation 19:20).

Being cast alive into the lake of fire is quite a contrast to the role of power and dominion the False Prophet and Antichrist enjoyed during the Tribulation. As Judge of all the earth, the Lord Jesus Christ consigns them to their fate when He returns to earth at the end of the Tribulation period. The devil, after being bound for a thousand years during the Millennium, will then join them in the lake of fire (Revelation 20:10).

It is not just the False Prophet who is judged—all those who took the mark of the Antichrist upon their bodies will suffer a similar judgment (Revelation 14:9-11; 16:1-2). Revelation makes clear that those who refuse the mark will be honored with eternal life (Revelation 20:4). Jesus' words in Matthew 10:28 will prove to be true: "And do not fear those who kill the body but cannot kill the soul. But rather fear Him who is able to destroy both soul and body in hell."

Notes

1. John Phillips, *Exploring Revelation: An Expository Commentary* (Grand Rapids, MI: Kregel Publications, 1987), 171.
2. Donald Grey Barnhouse, *Revelation: An Expository Commentary* (Grand Rapids, MI: Zondervan, 1971), 240.
3. Robert H. Mounce, *The New International Commentary on the New Testament: The Book of Revelation* (Grand Rapids, MI: Wm. B. Eerdmans Publishing Co., 1998), 255.
4. W. A. Criswell, *Expository Sermons on Revelation*, Vol. 4, 115-16.
5. Craig S. Keener, *The NIV Application Commentary: Revelation* (Grand Rapids, MI: Zondervan, 2009), 357.
6. Henry Morris, *The Revelation Record* (Wheaton, IL: Tyndale House Publishers, 1963), 251.
7. Fredrick A. Tatford, *Prophecy's Last Word: An Exposition of the Revelation* (London: Pickering & Ingles Ltd., 1947), 154.
8. Donald Grey Barnhouse, *Revelation: An Expository Commentary* (Grand Rapids, MI: Zondervan Publishing House, 1978), 250.

PERSONAL QUESTIONS

1. In Revelation 16:13, why is it fair to refer to the three figures mentioned as an "unholy trinity"?

   a. Moving from left to right, draw lines connecting the members of the unholy trinity to their biblical identities and to their parallel figures in the Holy Trinity:

   Biblical Names of the

Unholy Trinity	Unholy Trinity	Holy Trinity
• the Dragon	• the False Prophet	• God the Father
• the Beast	• Satan	• God the Holy Spirit
• the False Prophet	• the Antichrist	• God the Son

   b. What does Leviticus 11:10, 41 say about the clean or unclean nature of frogs?

   c. What is the point of unclean creatures coming out of the mouth in Revelation 16:13? (What is the mouth's primary function?) What will the world hear from these three creatures when they speak?

d. In John's vision of Christ returning, what is coming out of Christ's mouth? (Revelation 19:15) What is meant by a sword coming from the mouth of Christ instead of the sword being in His hand?

e. How does the Word of God "judge" us if we are sensitive to it? (Hebrews 4:12)

2. What outward demeanor is suggested by the vision of the False Prophet as a lamb? (Revelation 13:11)

a. Why is this "gentle" image appropriate for one who will pose as a spiritual leader?

b. What is the ultimate goal of a false prophet? (Matthew 24:11)

The Beast From the Earth • 125

GROUP QUESTIONS

1. Why is the False Prophet pictured as a lamb if he is actually a deceiver? (Matthew 7:15)

   a. What will the False Prophet use to deceive people into believing he is from God? (Matthew 24:24)

   b. What does that say about "power" as a sign of spiritual authenticity? Why is character more important than power? (What determines how power will be used?)

   c. How does John say Christians should respond to demonstrations of power? (1 John 4:1)

d. What kind of tests would reveal the nature of someone demonstrating spiritual power or authority? (See, for example, 1 John 4:2-3.)

e. Why is a spiritual leader's opinion of Christ always the definitive test?

2. What should you do when encountering a seemingly powerful spiritual leader about whom you have doubts?

DID YOU KNOW?

Throughout history people have sought to connect the number 666 by *gematria*—assigning numerical value to letters, words, or phrases. Using this and related methods, the number 666 has been linked to historical figures such as the Roman Emperor Nero, Muhammad, Hitler, some American politicians, and various Popes through the ages. Obviously, all those connections have proved to be false. A parallel to 666 on the hand and forehead may be the Jewish custom of binding the Word of God in small packets on the back of the hand and the forehead to honor the Word of God (Deuteronomy 6:8). The mark of the Antichrist on hand and forehead would be in direct contrast—honoring the commands of man rather than of God.

LESSON 21

MARTYRS
THE MARTYRS

Revelation 6:9-11

In this lesson we discover the fate of those who embrace Christ during the Tribulation and are martyred for their faith.

OUTLINE

Throughout history there have been many who gave up their lives rather than deny their faith in God. And there will be many more. During the seven-year Tribulation, there will be many who are killed because of their allegiance to Christ, for which they will be eternally rewarded.

I. The Context of Their Martyrdom

II. The Cause of Their Martyrdom

III. The Consequence of Their Martyrdom

IV. The Cry of Their Martyrdom

V. The Comfort of Their Martyrdom
   A. They Are Given a Refuge
   B. They Are Given a Robe
   C. They Are Given a Rest
   D. They Are Given Retribution
   E. They Are Given a Reward

VI. The Courage of Martyrdom

OVERVIEW

The third century Church father, Tertullian, wrote, "The blood of the martyrs is the seed [of the church]." By that, he meant that the more the Church is persecuted and Christians are killed, the more the Church grows. In spite of all the attempts throughout history to persecute the people of God, more and more are added.

The Pharaoh of Egypt tried to kill all male babies when they were born to keep the Hebrew slaves from multiplying. The wicked Persian official, Haman, devised a plan to exterminate all the Jews in Persia (following the Babylonian captivity). In the second century before Christ, Antiochus Epiphanes, a Seleucid king in the Middle East, persecuted the Jews who had returned from Babylon. Herod tried to kill Christ by murdering Jewish males under two years of age. John the Baptist was beheaded. The apostle James was beheaded. Following Pentecost, Jewish officials put many Jewish Christians to death. Many other Christians were persecuted and killed all over the Roman Empire for their faith. Many post-Reformation Christians in Europe were persecuted for breaking from the Catholic Church. Untold numbers of Christians have died in the modern era in China and Russia.

So intense was Hitler's persecution of the Jews in Europe that the Jewish population of the world was reduced to probably less than the number of Jews who left Egypt under Moses. In Germany, in 1938, almost 600 synagogues were destroyed within a few days. The windows of every Jewish establishment had been shattered. In the Buchenwald concentration camp, the death rate was 30 percent of the inmates. Similar conditions prevailed in concentration camps in Sachsenhausen and Dachau. The Auschwitz camp was equipped to execute 10,000 Jews per day. In Treblinka, another of Hitler's torture camps, 25,000 per day could be destroyed. The infamous Adolf Eichmann expressed Nazi hatred for the Jews: "I shall leap into my grave, for the thought that I have five million lives on my conscience is to me a source of inordinate satisfaction."[1]

The prediction of Moses concerning the Jews has literally been fulfilled throughout Jewish history:

"Then the Lord will scatter you among all peoples, from one end of the earth to the other, and there you shall serve other gods, which neither you nor your fathers have known—wood and stone. And among those nations you shall find no rest, nor shall the sole of your foot have a resting place; but there the Lord will give you a trembling heart, failing eyes, and anguish of soul. Your life shall hang in doubt before you; you shall fear day and night, and have no assurance of life. In the morning you shall say, 'Oh, that it were evening!' And at evening you shall say, 'Oh, that it were morning!' because of the fear which terrifies your heart, and because of the sight which your eyes see" (Deuteronomy 28:64-67).

In spite of all that, the number of Jews and Christians continues to increase. But the apostle John tells us that suffering and martyrdom has not ended; there will be more martyrs in the future during the Tribulation. From what John saw in his revelation from Jesus Christ, we can know who they are, how they will suffer, and how they will be preserved and rewarded by God.

THE CONTEXT OF THEIR MARTYRDOM

The most important contextual fact is that the Church of Jesus Christ has been removed from earth; after the Rapture, there will be no Christians on planet earth. So the martyrs are non-Christians at the beginning of the Tribulation who hear the Gospel and believe—and are subsequently martyred for their faith.

John sees the martyrs in heaven calling out for judgment on those who had killed them on earth, so their persecutors were still alive (Revelation 6:10). These saints were martyred in the early part of the Tribulation (included among those seen in Revelation 15:2).

During the Tribulation God will deal once again with Israel, and many Jews will turn to Him. Paul writes in Romans 11:25-26 that after "the fullness of the Gentiles has come in . . . all Israel will be saved." Paul anticipates the fulfillment of the prophecy in Isaiah 59:20, which is echoed in Romans 11:26: "The Deliverer will come out of Zion, and He will turn away ungodliness from Jacob." God will remove the blindness from Israel's eyes (Isaiah 6:9-10; Matthew 13:13-15), and she will recognize Christ as her Messiah and believe. But the price for that faith will be high; the Antichrist will murder many.

People will be saved during the Tribulation through various means: the two witnesses (Revelation 11:3), the 144,000 Jewish evangelists (Revelation 7:4), and by reading copies of the Word of God and other Christian books that they will find all over the world. Dr. Henry M. Morris has written,

"Millions upon millions of copies of the Bible and Bible portions have been published in all major languages, and distributed throughout the world through the dedicated ministries of the Gideons, the Wycliffe Bible Translators, and other such Christian organizations. Removal of believers from the world at the rapture will not remove the Scriptures, and multitudes will no doubt be constrained to read the Bible in those days. . . . Thus, multitudes will turn to their Creator and Savior in those days, and will be willing to give their testimony for the Word of God and even to give their lives as they seek to persuade the world that the calamities it is suffering are judgments from the Lord."[2]

Many will be called upon during the Tribulation to love God more than their very lives (Revelation 12:11; see also Psalm 44:22). They will be called to emulate the commitment of Shadrach, Meshach, and Abed-Nego—the young Hebrew men in Babylon who refused to bow down to the king's idol: "Let it be known to you, O king, that we do not serve your gods, nor will we worship the gold image which you have set up" (Daniel 3:17-18). And the commitment of New Testament martyrs as well: John the Baptist (Mark 6:14-29), Stephen (Acts 7), those killed by Saul of Tarsus (Acts 8:3; 9:1), James (Acts 12:1-2), and Antipas (Revelation 2:13). Jesus warned His followers of the possibility of death (Matthew 24:9; Luke 21:12-19). The prophet Zechariah wrote that a day was coming when two-thirds of the population of Israel would be "cut off." The remaining third would be brought through the fire and refined (Zechariah 13:8-9). And Jesus described this coming bloodshed in His sermon on the Mount of Olives: "Then they will deliver you up to tribulation and kill you, and you will be hated by all nations for My name's sake" (Matthew 24:8-10).

Scholar Richard Bauckham has clarified: The book of Revelation doesn't say every living Christian on earth will be killed in the Tribulation. "But [Revelation] does require that every faithful Christian must be prepared to die."[3]

THE CAUSE OF THEIR MARTYRDOM

The martyrs are killed "for the word of God and for the testimony which they held" (Revelation 6:9)—the same reasons John himself was exiled to Patmos (Revelation 1:9). Their "testimony" is likely the message of coming judgment that they preach, warning others to repent and be saved. In spreading such a message, these Tribulation saints will join other biblical heroes who preached the same message: Samuel, Isaiah, Jeremiah, Jonah, and the rest of the prophets.

The word "slain" (Revelation 6:9), used to describe the killing of the martyrs, is always used by the apostle John to refer to the killing of Christ or His followers (one exception: Revelation 13:3). It could easily be translated "slaughtered," "butchered," or "murdered," as when it was used in the context of sacrificial animals. John means to emphasize the brutal nature of these martyrs' deaths.

THE CONSEQUENCE OF THEIR MARTYRDOM

The fact that John saw the souls of the martyrs "under the altar" (Revelation 6:9) is a reference to their blood being spilled as a sacrifice for the cause of Christ. This calls to mind the practice of the priests in the Old Testament who would pour some sacrificial blood *on* the altar and pour the remainder *under* (at the base of) the altar: "You shall take some of the blood of the bull and put it on the horns of the altar with your finger, and pour all the blood beside the base of the altar" (Exodus 29:12). Being under the altar of God pictures the martyrs as having sacrificed their blood (their life) for Christ.

THE CRY OF THEIR MARTYRDOM

The martyrs cry out, "How long, O Lord, holy and true, until You judge and avenge our blood on those who dwell on the earth?" (Revelation 6:10). This is another piece of evidence that these martyrs are not from the Church Age where calling for vengeance on one's enemies would be improper (Romans 12:17-19). Instead, the correct response toward one's murderers would be that of Stephen: "Lord, do not charge them with this sin" (Acts 7:60; see also Romans 12:20-21).

The martyrs of the Tribulation period are not living in the age of grace; they were living in a period of judgment by God upon His enemies on earth. An imprecatory prayer will be highly appropriate in that day. Louis T. Talbot has said this about the martyrs' cry for vengeance:

"A man prays according to the attitude God is taking toward the world in the dispensation in which he lives. This present age is the age of grace. God is showing grace and mercy to the worst of men, and we are told to pray for them that despitefully use us. But in the tribulation period God will be meting out judgment upon the earth."[4]

THE COMFORT OF THEIR MARTYRDOM

"Then a white robe was given to each of them; and it was said to them that they should rest a little while longer, until both the number of their fellow servants and their brethren, who would be killed as they were, was completed" (Revelation 6:11). It is amazing to think about "resting" while waiting for other martyrs on earth to be "killed as they were." But that is the rest that accompanies being secure in the will of a sovereign God.

They Are Given a Refuge

"Under the altar" (Revelation 6:9) serves as an image of safety and protection. It conveys the idea that the redeemed, regardless of what their earthly experience has been, are safe in the presence of God.

Dr. Donald Grey Barnhouse reminds us:

"We are not to think that John had a vision of an altar with souls peeping out from underneath. The whole teaching of the Old Testament is that the altar was the place of the sacrifice of blood. To be 'under the altar' is to be covered in the sight of God by that merit which Jesus Christ provided in dying on the cross. It is a figure that speaks of justification. . . . These martyred witnesses are covered by the work of the Lord Jesus Christ."[5]

They Are Given a Robe

Each of the Jewish martyrs "under the altar" was given a white robe to wear (Revelation 6:11). Generally speaking, the white robe is a sign of righteousness (Revelation 19:8). But the very notion of a robe, being a garment, raises this question: What kind of a body do the martyrs have in heaven? They will not receive their own resurrection bodies until the end of the Tribulation. So what is their form until then?

Dr. John Walvoord addresses this question:

"The martyred dead here pictured have not been raised from the dead and have not received their resurrection bodies. Yet it is declared that they are given robes. This would almost demand that they have a body of some kind. A robe could not hang upon an immaterial soul or spirit. It is not the kind of body that Christians now have, that is the body of the earth, nor is it the resurrection body of flesh and bones of which Christ spoke after His own resurrection. It is a temporary body suited for their presence in heaven but replaced in turn by their everlasting resurrection body given at the time of Christ's return."[6]

They Are Given a Rest

When the martyrs ask how long it will be until they are avenged for their death, they are told to rest for a little while "until both the number of their fellow servants and their brethren, who would be killed as they were, was completed" (Revelation 6:11). That is, God's judgment would be forestalled "a little while longer" before it could be fully realized.

There are two primary times of Jewish martyrdom during the Tribulation—here, under the fifth seal judgment (Revelation 6:9), and a second period yet to come. Until the second period of persecution and martyrdom is complete, God will withhold His judgment. In the interim, the martyrs are told to rest: "Write: 'Blessed are the dead who die in the Lord from now on.' 'Yes,' says the Spirit, 'that they may rest from their labors, and their works follow them'" (Revelation 14:13).

They Are Given Retribution

Finally, retribution is realized:

"Then another angel came out of the temple which is in heaven, he also having a sharp sickle. And another angel came out from the altar, who had power over fire, and he cried with a loud cry to him who had the sharp sickle, saying, 'Thrust in your sharp sickle and gather the clusters of the vine of the earth, for her grapes are fully ripe.' So the angel thrust his sickle into the earth and gathered the vine of the earth, and threw it into the great winepress of the wrath of God. And the winepress was trampled outside the city, and blood came out of the winepress, up to the horses' bridles, for one thousand six hundred furlongs" (Revelation 14:17-20).

The martyrs cried out to be avenged from the altar in heaven. From that same altar the angel of judgment is sent to avenge them in judgment.

They Are Given a Reward

For being faithful through a brief time of persecution and pain on earth, the martyrs are rewarded with a thousand years of reigning with Christ on earth:

"And I saw thrones, and they sat on them, and judgment was committed to them. Then I saw the souls of those who had been beheaded for their witness to Jesus and for the word of God, who had not worshiped the beast or his image, and had not received his mark on their foreheads or on their hands. And they lived and reigned with Christ for a thousand years" (Revelation 20:4).

The martyred saints will be honored in heaven forever; but even before that, they will be honored on earth as they live and reign with Christ during His Millennial reign.

All who pay the ultimate price for faithfulness to Christ throughout history will gain the everlasting reward of righteousness and fellowship with Him forever.

The Courage of Martyrdom

When we think of Christian martyrdom, we tend to think of the many stories of ancient witnesses who sacrificed their lives for their beliefs. But martyrdom isn't just in ancient history; Christians around the world today are still suffering martyrdom as well.

In the summer of 2005, two young Bangladeshi men showed the Jesus film to guests in their home. They were threatened with death if they did not cease the showings. When they did not comply, they were attacked in the dead of night and killed. Stories like this are not rare. Around the world today, Christians are experiencing persecution and death for their faith.

As we can see from history and current events today, persecution and martyrdom are the norm for the Christian. These martyrs—past, present, and future—provide ample examples of courage that should inspire us to a deeper commitment to Christ and a determination to stand strong for Him, no matter the cost.

Notes

1. Jacob Presser, *The Destruction of the Dutch Jews* (New York: Dutton, 1969), 336.
2. Henry M. Morris, *The Revelation Record* (Wheaton, IL: Tyndale House Publishers, Inc., 1983), 119.
3. Richard Bauckham, *Climax of Prophecy—Studies in the Book of Revelation* (Edinburgh: T. & Agents of the Apocalypse Study Guide, Lesson 2 The Martyrs Page 8 of 8 T. Clark, 1993), 424-25.
4. Louis T. Talbot, *The Revelation of Jesus Christ* (Grand Rapids: Wm. B. Eerdman's, 1937), 99.
5. Donald Grey Barnhouse, *Revelation: An Expository Commentary* (Grand Rapids: Zondervan, 1971), 134.
6. John F. Walvoord, *The Revelation of Jesus Christ* (Chicago: Moody Press, 1966), 134-135.

PERSONAL QUESTIONS

1. God told Israel they would endure times of persecution and trouble (Deuteronomy 28:64-67). But what would be the cause of that trouble? (Deuteronomy 28:58)

   a. So at least one reason for persecution can be_____.

   b. How would you explain the persecution and martyrdom of those mentioned in Hebrews 11:35-38?

   c. So another reason for persecution can be_____.

The Martyrs • 137

d. Into which of those two categories do the Tribulation martyrs fall?

e. Compare Hebrews 11:39-40 with Revelation 2:17. What is the end result for those who suffer for their faith?

2. What is the primary reason a Christian would be martyred? (Revelation 6:9)

GROUP QUESTIONS

1. Read Luke 14:25-35 and discuss the following questions:

    a. What serious condition does Jesus establish for any who want to follow Him? (Luke 14:27)

    b. Compare verse 27 with verse 33. In addition to material things, what else is included in the "all" in verse 33 (in light of "cross" in verse 27)?

    c. What is Jesus' point in verses 28-33? Why should martyrdom be considered a possible cost for following Christ?

d. What do Jesus' final words (last words of verse 35) suggest about taking up one's "cross" and "count[ing] the cost?" Why might some Christians not "hear" this message? (See for example, John 6:66.)

e. Why is risking martyrdom for Christ's sake still a good idea? (John 6:67-68)

f. How long were you a Christian before you realized the implications of taking up your "cross"? How many new Christians are encouraged to "count the cost" of following Jesus?

g. How do you think you would respond to the threat of martyrdom for your faith?

h. How does John 15:13 fit into the martyrdom equation? Is Jesus our "friend"? (see verse 14) What would be the greatest act of love for Jesus we could show?

DID YOU KNOW?

Technically, an imprecation is a spoken curse. An imprecation can be issued in the form of a request when one prays that God would curse, or judge, His enemies (the enemies of His people). Revelation 6:10 contains an imprecatory prayer offered by the Tribulation martyrs: "How long . . . until You judge . . . those who dwell on the earth?" Imprecatory prayers were common in the Old Testament, specifically in the Psalms (35, 40, 69, 79, 83, 109, 139, 143). Imprecatory prayers were not personal; the prayer was not offered out of frustration or a desire for personal revenge or vengeance. They were based on a desire for God's honor to be defended and restored, for His name to be vindicated. Vengeance and justice are always God's to pursue, not ours, as the New Testament teaches (Romans 12:17-21).

ADDITIONAL RESOURCES
by Dr. David Jeremiah

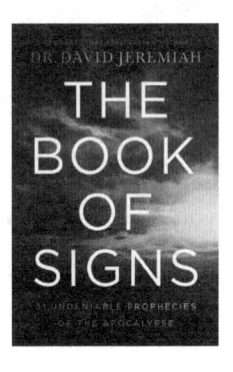

THE BOOK OF SIGNS
A compilation of years of study by Dr. Jeremiah, *The Book of Signs* will increase your understanding of prophecy and the End Times as Dr. Jeremiah explains 31 signs of the coming Apocalypse. Scripture contains multiple prophecies about the end of the age, and *The Book of Signs* will help you gain greater insight into many of these prophecies, so you can be prepared and guide others to the truths found in the Bible.

ESCAPE THE COMING NIGHT
Tragedy and violence surround us . . . political debates divide our society . . . our world seems to be coming apart at the seams. So is there any hope for peace in our time? In *Escape the Coming Night,* Dr. David Jeremiah narrates the book of Revelation, answering this question and more, for those who are willing to listen to what God declares about the final days and His coming reign.

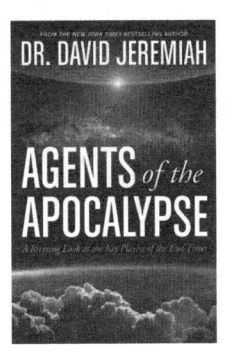

AGENTS OF THE APOCALYPSE

What if the players of the End Times were out in force today? In *Agents of the Apocalypse,* Dr. Jeremiah explores Revelation through the lens of its major players and reveals the overarching truth of Revelation—that the Christian's victory in Christ is an absolute certainty. He opens each chapter with a dramatization and ends each with "The Scripture Behind the Story," explaining how we should interpret and apply Revelation to our lives today.

AGENTS OF BABYLON

Babylon has been a symbol of evil since the beginning of time. And nowhere in the Bible can we see this exemplified more than in the book of Daniel. In *Agents of Babylon,* Dr. Jeremiah brings the characters and prophecies of Daniel to life, projecting them into the future to show us how to live in the present and have hope as these end-time events unfold.

Each of these resources was created from a teaching series by Dr. David Jeremiah. Contact Turning Point for more information about correlating materials.

For pricing information and ordering, contact us at

P.O. Box 3838
San Diego, CA 92163
(800) 947-1993
www.DavidJeremiah.org

STAY CONNECTED
to Dr. David Jeremiah

Take advantage of two great ways to let Dr. David Jeremiah give you spiritual direction every day!

Turning Points Magazine and Devotional

Receive Dr. David Jeremiah's magazine, *Turning Points*, each month:

- Thematic study focus
- 48 pages of life-changing reading
- Relevant articles
- Special features
- Daily devotional readings
- Bible study resource offers
- Live event schedule
- Radio & television information

Request *Turning Points* magazine today!
(800) 947-1993 | DavidJeremiah.org/Magazine

Daily Turning Point E-Devotional

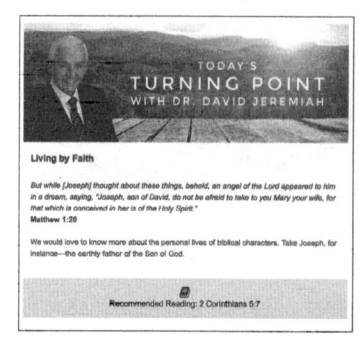

Start your day off right! Find words of inspiration and spiritual motivation waiting for you on your computer every morning! Receive a daily e-devotion communication from David Jeremiah that will strengthen your walk with God and encourage you to live the authentic Christian life.

Request your free e-devotional today!
(800) 947-1993
www.DavidJeremiah.org/Devo